HOT DIVE

By

JIM C. PRENTICE

Hot Dive

By

Jim C Prentice

ISBN 978-1-895903-15-7

Keystone Publications

DEDICATION

This book is dedicated first and foremost to my Comrades In Arms of all nations, friend and foe. It is not, has never been, nor ever will be our choice to take up arms against each other. Our lives have, and always will be, the pawns played by the politics, religions, and beliefs of those in command. To those acting on their own behalf to inflict harm or damage for the pure sake of terror I offer no respite. Your end will come. To those Comrades still alive, and to those that have passed before us, I can only say this:

"ThankYou Brother".

I would be remiss if I did not mention my loving wife of 53years without whose patience and sacrifices I would never have become a writer. I also thank three generations of descendents for their love and support in all areas of family activities. For my daughters, grand-children, great-grand-children of the present and those yet unborn I wish you peace, hope, love, and prosperity. -

Chapter One

In the open country of central Afghanistan heat, sand, dust, rocks and more sand offered little shelter or protection to the troops.

Dive team "Alpha" had driven two hours north of Kabul to reach today's search area. In the distance they could hear bombs and artillery fire accompanied by the brief staccato bursts of small arms fire.

The double edged sword of war becomes obvious to those faced with disarming or destroying munitions. Whether it be Improvised Explosive Devices (IEDs) placed by the enemy or Unexploded Bombs (UXBs)and live artillery shells from allied action, the results are just as deadly.

The hill country around them presented danger from enemy guns and mortars. But their greatest threat was from small, heavily armed, roving patrols.

Often it was hard to tell terrorists from peaceful civilians until they exposed their weapons. Their only chance for survival was a constant vigil, their weapons at the ready to instantly return fire when needed. The nerve-wracking threat of suicide bombers was ever-present. They had seen the enemy carrying explosives on foot, on bicycles, and in vehicles attempting to approach close enough to kill the unaware, the innocent bystanders, and the unlucky troops.

The dive team, composed of Royal Canadian

Engineers and an infantry protection platoon from the Royal Canadian Regiment were assigned to clear and secure bridges over rivers, highway overpasses and other strategically placed structures.

Terrorists, either while retreating, or hiding by day as peaceful citizens, plant and leave behind explosive devices. Each day our troops face explosions with deadly results. One of the most dangerous missions is the underwater examination of bridges, piers, and harbor docks. Many of these structures are booby-trapped with explosives and some are watched over by heavily armed and well hidden enemy troops.

The dive team was nearly finished inspecting a bridge near Kabul when the distant war came to them.

* * * *

With their diver in the water the tenders on the surface were watchful. Eyes constantly roving they searched for any sign of trouble, either in the water or out. Although their first concern was the safety of the man in the water, they must also be aware of surface threats from enemy forces, mines and booby-traps.

Below the surface the diver, armed only with a diving knife, inspected every foot of the old concrete bridge. Visibility in the murky water was limited to less than a meter so it was slow and tedious. He searched not only for the obvious bulky packages of high explosives but also for wires to detonators, instantaneous fuse, or other munitions.

He carried a series of red floats on long strings to mark any devices he found. It was a risky job. The constant possibility of tripping a booby trap was bad enough but the country was full of unexploded bombs. Just a nudge could be enough to trigger an explosion from any one of them.

He checked his tank pressure gauge. Working in the warm and shallow water allowed him more time submerged than usual but within a few minutes he would have to surface for a new tank. His tender crew watched his bubble stream as he approached the final bridge support. The job was nearly done.

Their machine gunner slowly spun the cupola on top of their vehicle, watching for any threatening behaviour along the river bank while traversing the .50 caliber weapon. The RG-31 Nyala wheeled armoured vehicle was new to Afghanistan but it had proven itself many times over as the best fighting vehicle available.

Behind a wall at the end of the bridge another team was preparing to complete their task. The Taliban terrorists, dressed as civilians, carried rifles and rocket propelled grenades. As one man prepared to fire an RPG the others took up defensive positions where they could add their fire to support the pending grenade attack. Their main target was the armored vehicle. If they could disable it the Canadians would be unable to escape. With additional grenades and sniping with their AK-47assault rifles they could kill the entire dive detachment.

The grenade team picked a tough target. Unfamiliar with the tank-like Nyala, they were unaware of the nearly bomb-proof armour. It was very unlikely the RPG would disable it.

As the Taliban with the launcher raised his weapon above the wall he caught the attention of the ever alert Canadian gunner. He was pulling the trigger when one of the bullets from the .50 caliber machine gun hit the wall in front of him. The ricochet struck him under the chin. He was dead before he hit the ground.

Despite the incoming rocket, the gunner continued his fire while the surprised Taliban tried to flee to the safety of the village buildings. Two more died as they scurried for safety.

The remaining Canadians joined the defense, ever watchful for another attack. The grenade missed the

Nyala, striking the bridge support behind it.

His air exhausted, the diver had just surfaced and was climbing the embankment. With an ear-splitting bang the RPG struck the wall behind the Nyala near the rubber suited diver.

The explosion attracted the attention of the Dive-Master. Glancing back at the bridge he saw the blood-spattered body of his diver fall back into the river. An instant later he had shed his helmet and his body arced as he made a shallow dive toward the water.

"Diver is hit!" he shouted as his feet left the ground.

The remainder of the dive tending team reacted immediately, already the river ran red with blood. The bridge bore witness as blood ran down the shattered concrete. After pulling the unconscious diver ashore they began applying emergency field dressings to stem the flow. The Taliban and the war were now forgotten while they fought to save their comrade. He needed immediate medical care beyond the meager supplies in the Nyala.

* * * *

Several kilometres away the medical team of a Forward Medical Aid Station had set up shop in a deep wadi. The ravine-like depression offered protection from direct enemy fire while providing cover for the defensive fire team tasked with their protection.

In the large tent there were three doctors, four male and two female nurses, and several orderlies. Together they prepared for the inevitable casualties. They would treat the wounded from both sides.

Janice Northwaite was preoccupied with preparing the triage area and readying the stretchers. Her tour was coming to an end and she was daydreaming about the snow waiting for her at home. She had seen enough of war, sand, rocks, heat and death! There seemed to be no end to the stream of mangled and bleeding bodies. The lucky ones went home on a stretcher or a wheel chair. The rest traveled in a box on a cargo plane.

Her replacement had already arrived and was up to speed with the job. Janice waited for the opportunity to get a ride back to Kabul. Then a long flight home and her war was over.

The roar of the Nyala engine announced its arrival before it came into sight, instinctively she knew what was about to occur.

"Heads up troops!" She called, while donning a pair of surgical gloves.

A cloud of dust and sand followed the vehicle as it entered the wadi. After skidding to a halt near the tent several soldiers lifted a buddy and carried him to a waiting stretcher. Jan winced at the blood tinged field dressings.

A strange black rubber suit trickled blood from numerous slashes around an assortment of wounds. Janice tried to smile to hide her initial reaction. This one would have to be very lucky not to be in a box by nightfall.

The station team worked through the afternoon and into the evening trying to keep him alive. He had to be reasonably stable to survive the flight to a rear echelon hospital. Sunrise found Jan outside taking a break when the helicopter arrived.

"Corporal Northwaite!" The head surgeon was shouting at her. "Get your kit and get on that helo. This soldier is your ticket home. Good bye, good luck, and thank you."

It took but a microsecond for her brain to process the order. The orderlies loaded the wounded diver into the aircraft while Jan grabbed her gear. Within minutes they were airborne, bound for the field hospital in Kabul.

* * * *

"What the hell?" muttered Hal Sigurdson as he regained consciousness. The roar of aircraft engines assaulted his ears and added to his pounding headache. He nearly screamed from the excruciating pain in his leg. Opening his eyes and he recognized the interior of the C-130 Hercules military cargo plane.

He was strapped to a stretcher, unable to move. Looking around he noticed black spots floating before his eyes. His stomach roiled in protest. Already he regretted his damned curiosity and closed his eyes.

"Well hi there, and welcome back!" The feminine voice came from above his head. He twisted to see where the voice was coming from. A woman, dressed in camouflage combat gear, stepped up beside him.

"What happened?" he growled.

The young woman smiled and replied. "I won't ask you how you feel because I know you are going through hell. Now that you're awake, I'll get you something to ease the pain. Can you tell me your name and rank? And what you do?"

Hal nearly swore at the woman. She's a nurse, he thought. She's doing her job, trying to help. "Sigurdson," he blurted, trying to be heard above the noise of the four big turbo-prop engines. "Warrant Officer Harry L. Sigurdson, but my friends call me Hal." Even talking hurt his chest; it felt like he had some broken ribs. "I'm part of an underwater reconnaissance and demolition team. I was checking a bridge, and that's the last thing I remember."

"Okay Warrant Officer Sigurdson, may I call you Hal?"

Hal nodded. "Sure! But where are we going?"

"One last question, what is your date of birth?"

"January sixth, seventy five," he mumbled, getting

annoyed again by her questions.

She made several notes on her clipboard. "Thanks," she replied, entering his age as thirty-seven on the chart before reaching for a medical kit. "Now let me give you that shot, then I'll try to answer your questions." She kept up the conversation while preparing a syringe.

"My name is Master Corporal Janice Northwaite. I'm a Canadian Army nurse and I'm here to care for you until we arrive at the airport in Frankfurt, Germany. There you'll receive more advanced care than we could provide in Kabul." She pulled down the sheet and swabbed his arm with alcohol. "Just a little pin-prick." She warned as the needle went in." There, that should help in a few minutes. Do you remember anything from before the explosion?"

He turned his head from her to gaze at the bottom of the stretcher rack above his. ""Not really," he said. "I was in the water checking for explosives or damage to the bridge when there was a roar and I guess I blacked out. The next thing I know I was here with you asking me questions. Hey how about my guys? Is the rest of the crew okay?"

"From what I gathered from your buddies you were under the last bridge support. You were leaving the water when your team came under attack. Apparently the Taliban launched a rocket-propelled grenade at your vehicle but it missed. Instead it hit the bridge right beside you. Your legs, hip, and hand took the worst of it. But you also have some nasty RPG shrapnel and concrete fragments in your side. Your buddies are okay! They took some flesh wounds but stayed in Kabul. Right now let's see if we can make you a bit more comfortable." She unbuckled the top straps over his arms and chest and loosened the lower ones on his hips and legs.

Hal tried to look at his watch. Then he noticed the IV needle in his right arm. The plastic tubes led to several bags of fluid hanging overhead. His diving watch was missing.

Jan noticed his expression and responded, "Your watch is here in your pack with the rest of your kit. Would you like to put it back on?"

"Yes, please," replied the wounded diver. "How long have I been out?"

Jan pulled the watch from his bag and helped him strap it on. "You were unconscious when they brought you to the forward aid station. That was two days ago. You were still out cold when we reached the field hospital. They kept you sedated while they did what they could to close the wounds and stabilize you for the flight. We've been in the air for almost three hours. We have to make a fuel stop and then on to Germany. So, are you hungry or thirsty? Can I get you anything?"

"I'm dry as hell, I'm hungry, and my teeth are covered with fur," he responded.

"I'll be right back" Jan turned and headed for the flight deck. She needed to inform the Captain that their critical passenger had finally regained consciousness. There were eleven other wounded Canadians aboard the Medical Evacuation flight but Sigurdson was the worst. Since she had brought him in from the field, and she was going home anyway, she had been assigned to him for the flight. There were four other nurses caring for the rest of the wounded.

As the flight droned on, Hal drank apple juice and munched on a sandwich. The morphine had taken effect but the pain had not completely disappeared.

When he awoke again, he was in an ambulance, Jan was no longer by his side. A young guy in hospital whites with Sergeant's stripes on his collar had replaced her.

The EMT, noticing Hal was awake, asked "How

do you feel?"

"I feel like I've been run over by a cement truck."

The sergeant smiled, "Is that better or worse than getting hit by a grenade?"

"I don't know," quipped Hal. " But now I know how a tank feels when a grenade hits it."

Thankfully the ride to the hospital was a short one. No longer on a stretcher, the rolling gurney was a little more comfortable. Hal felt a bit dizzy, lightheaded, and sleepy from the morphine.

The next time he awoke his left foot was aching and itching at the same time. He moved his right foot over to scratch the itch.

He couldn't find his foot!

Hal sat bolt upright, staring at the foot of the bed. Where his foot should have been the covers showed only the outline of his lower leg. With a mighty heave he tore the covers loose, exposing his legs. Then, flopping back onto the pillow, he became painfully aware that his violent reaction had torn the IV from his arm. The increase in heart rate and blood pressure triggered an alarm. The machines connected to him began to beep.

Within seconds a nurse was at his side. She spotted the hanging IV needle and the blood on the sheet under his arm.

"What happened?" she asked.

"My foot!" He shouted, much louder than necessary. "I don't have a foot!"

The nurse quieted the alarms and checked his dressings before she left. A few moments later she returned and inserted a new IV needle.

It would take a long time to get used to having pain in a foot that he did not have.

"A Phantom Pain." That's what the doctors called it.

* * * *

He spent four weeks in a U.S. Army hospital in Germany. After several operations the staff decided he was well enough to travel. He endured a long and boring flight back to Canada. It had now been four months since the grenade attack struck him down. Finally coming to terms with his injuries he now accepted the fact that he had lost his left foot and two fingers on his left hand. Hideous red scars adorned his legs, hips and chest. They were permanent reminders of how close to death he had come. But at least he was home. He was one of the lucky ones, alive, aware, and thankful,. He had watched too many friend's coffins being loaded onto a C-130 for the final ride home.

His life in the veteran's hospital became an endless torture of physiotherapy. He wondered if he would ever get used to having pain in a foot that was no longer there. At least now he had mastered the artificial foot and could walk fairly well. He exercised for two hours every morning and two hours each afternoon. His time was spent either in the hot tank at physiotherapy, walking on the treadmill, or doing laps in the indoor pool. He had come a long way but had a long way to go yet.

Autumn leaves now littered the ground and winter would soon arrive. The first snow had already put in an appearance.

With so much time on his hands Hal's mind worked overtime. An idea had popped into his head recently and wouldn't budge. That morning, when his doctor showed up for morning rounds, Hal propositioned him.

"Hey Doc, what's chances of getting out of here for a while?"

The doctor checked the notes on the clipboard on

the end of the bed as he replied. "To go where and do what?" he queried. "You need a lot more physiotherapy before you're anywhere near back in shape."

Hal's rehearsed reply flowed from his lips. "Doc I'm a diver, I'm used to open water. Doing laps in that pool is so damned monotonous I'm gonna go nuts. I figure I could go down to Mexico for the winter. I could spend my time exploring reefs in the Caribbean and walking jungle trails. The worst of my wounds are healing nicely and you said the risk of infection had passed. What better physiotherapy is there than four or five hours a day swimming in warm salt water?"

The doctor shoved his hands deep into the pockets of his white lab coat. He looked at Hal and cocked his head to one side. "Let me talk to your therapist," he said. "Then we'll check your blood work. It just might be a good plan."

Chapter Two

Aided by his swim-fins, Hal's fluttering kick slowly propelled him along the reef. He followed the outer edge of a drop-off, where the deeper waters began. Through the glass of his diving mask the beauty of the sea unfolded before him. A simple snorkel poked out of the water behind his head permitting him to breathe. The buoyancy effect of the salt water enabled him to glide with minimal effort along the coral. It had taken some time to get used to having a swim fin attached to his stump instead of the prosthetic foot.

The blue green waters of the bay rose and fell gently as the swells from the Caribbean rolled toward the glistening white sand of the beach.

Overhead the sun beat down on the water producing a dazzling display of reflected pinpoints on the wave tops. A few wispy white clouds marched overhead driven by a gentle southern breeze that also created a slight swaying in the palm trees along the shore.

His medium length sun-bleached blonde hair streamed out behind him. With easy strokes he propelled his six foot tanned and muscular body forward. With all the hospital rehabilitation he had regained most of his pre-accident fitness level.

The pristine coral reef, only a hundred yards offshore, lay just a few feet below the surface. Here, the sea fans waved with the timeless motion of the waves. In total unison thousands of them moved in perfect harmony. The seemingly senseless growth of coral polyps held no pattern or direction. Nor did they sway with the relentless waves. Each of the brownish-green sea fans carried several cowries. The shells of which made attractive jewelry for natives and tourists alike.

On this day Hal ignored the shells, they would be here another time. For now he was content to just cruise the reef and enjoy the view. Earlier he had been keeping track of the numbers and varieties of species of small fish living in and around the reef. He had soon lost count.

For a brief moment, he wished he had someone, preferably a female, to share this beauty with. The face of the nurse on the C-130 flashed across his mind. If a swimsuit fit her body as nicely as those combat fatigues, he'd accompany her on a dive every day for the rest of his life. Just wishful thinking, he told himself.

Like sparkling jewels the little fish flashed in the sunlight penetrating the shallow water. An endless scene of flashing colors reminded Hal of a boyhood toy he had enjoyed. The kaleidoscope was the only thing he could remember that produced such a vivid display. Most of the bigger fish were no bigger than his hand and the smaller ones were more the size of his thumb. Singly, and in small schools, they flashed various shades of yellow, blue, pink, and green as they darted among the coral.

Occasionally he saw the head and claws of a lobster protruding from a cave-like hole in the coral. He tried to make a mental note of the location of each of these crustaceans. Imagining them cooking on a fire on the beach he could almost taste them. He envisioned them dipped in drawn butter with a touch of dill and garlic.

Other, larger fish included groupers, moray eels, and redfish with an occasional cruising shark in the distance. The small spear gun he carried would be no match for a large attacking shark. Before leaving the water he hoped to spear a fish for his evening meal. His only real concern were the ever-present jellyfish drifting on the current. The thread-like appendages hanging below these gelatinous denizens produced burn-like welts after contacting bare skin. It was a painful experience he had felt before and did not want to repeat.

Ahead and to the right he could see a sea trout hanging motionless below a head shaped lump of coral. The water depth here was about ten feet to the bottom and about four feet to the top of the coral. He estimated the fish to be about six feet down.

Ready to go ashore, he decided this could be his supper. He pulled back the surgical rubber elastics to load the spear gun. Taking a deep breath, he held it, executed a gentle surface dive, and plunged slowly downward. As he descended Hal felt the change in water temperature, even a few feet made a difference.

Holding the spear gun out in front he glided downward, taking aim at the hovering trout. Being in such a remote area it had no reason to fear the strange creature descending from above. A length of stout line attached to the spear limited the range of the weapon. Hal waited until he was just a few feet above his prey, and then gently pulled the trigger.

Once released the metal rod took less than a second to strike the fish. Impaled on the barbed shaft; it could not possibly escape. Pulling in the few feet of line he soon had the spear with the still wriggling fish in his hand.

Yes! Hal shouted silently as he headed for the surface. Had there been an onlooker nearby they would have seen the fish suddenly appear out of the water. Supported by a thin silver shaft, it was followed immediately by a head. As Hal blew the water out of the flooded snorkel a silvery spout of water appeared over his head. He took a moment to admire the trout. Just a nice size for dinner, he thought, about three pounds. Now he could head back to shore.

Ahead of him, near the beach, an old tree trunk protruded from the water. Blackened by years in the sea and encrusted with barnacles it was Hal's marker for his entry point. Just below the surface a piece of brilliant blue fabric swayed in the swells. It was attached to the tree by the waist drawstring.

Hal retrieved the bit of fabric, kicked off his fins, and thrust his legs into it. He preferred to swim nude and this was his changing room. The feeling of freedom he enjoyed was one of the best parts of his forays along the reef. The warm water flowing over his buttocks and male parts was far more pleasant and natural than the confining bathing suit. Just once he had been caught exiting the water naked by a group of wandering tourists. That had been several years ago but they raised such a fuss that he now elected to wear a swimsuit to enter and leave the water.

Leaving the tree behind it was a short swim to shallower water where he could walk ashore on the sandy bottom. Aside from the fading scars there were no tan lines or white areas on his skin. A solid golden tan was evidence of the time he spent sunning nude on the remote beaches.

Partially hidden among the swaying palms his Chevy pickup waited patiently. The old truck, now in its twenty-fifth year, was in remarkably good condition. Indeed it had effortlessly made the journey from Canada, across the USA, and through Mexico to this favored spot. South of Cancun, in the state of Quintaneroo, it was near the border of Belize. Here he had found a haven of tropical beauty.

As he waded ashore his one bare foot burned on the hot sand. He was forced to increase his speed until he reached the cooling shade below the palms. He had still not gotten used to not having a left foot. As he approached his truck he noticed another vehicle parked up the beach.

He unlocked the door, opened a cooler and, extracted a cold can of beer. His favorite cervesa, or Mexican beer, was Pacifico, and he always had a few in his cooler. He preferred the light pilsner to the Corona lager that seemed to be the preference of most tourists.

After popping the tab and enjoying a big swallow he retrieved a lawn chair from the truck-mounted camper. By sitting it in a shady spot, he could enjoy the breeze and had a clear view up and down the beach.

The other vehicle appeared to be an older motor home. Near it he could see a woman. She was setting up a table, obviously preparing to stay for a while. She looked to be about his age, mid- thirties, tall, slim, dark hair, and nicely proportioned. She wore a white bikini and it accented a very nice tan. Hal admired her from his vantage point and wondered where her husband was. It was not often that another traveler happened upon this remote stretch of beach. Usually his only neighbors were the local Mexicans.

Chapter Three

After arriving home from Afghanistan Jan was diagnosed with Post Traumatic Stress Disorder. To help her deal with it her Commanding Officer had given her a chance for an extended leave. It would be up to her whether she wanted to continue her military career or return to a civilian job.

When asked about a husband she repeated the often-told yet false story. She explained that he had been killed in Afghanistan when a roadside mine exploded beside his vehicle. How it had been four years since his death and she was just now getting on with her life. Just as she had learned to be married and share her life with Dick, she now had to unlearn that part of here life and revert back to being single.

It was true that she and Dick had bought this older motor home not long after they were married. They both loved to travel and disliked staying in hotels every night. The old coach was in good shape with low mileage and they got it for a bargain price. Several times each year when Dick was not away on business trips or looking after business they went camping together.

He had convinced her to drive the bus-like RV and taught her how to do the routine maintenance it required. Now she was thankful he had.

For the past three years the coach had sat unused in a storage lot. She had almost sold it before deciding she could still enjoy its comforts. Also, it reminded her of the happy years and good times she had enjoyed with her ex-husband. Her military income allowed her to travel if she remained modest with her expenditures.

This beach was perfect! Not only was it remote and pristine, it was free. She could stay here for weeks if she wanted to. She would venture back to civilization only to dump the holding tanks, fill with water, top up the propane tank and buy groceries. The world was her oyster as her father would have said.

She withdrew most of her savings and had the bank convert the cash to travelers checks. After waiting patiently for three weeks herpassport finally arrived. So armed and prepared to face the world she headed south. By driving several hours each day it took nearly a week to cross the United States.

Some required shopping was completed in Pharr, Texas before crossing the Mexican border. By knowing where she was going she was able to travel the Autostrada, the Mexican equivalent of an Interstate. She was nearly a week crossing this country before arriving at a place of peace and solitude on the shore of the Carribean Sea.

On the beach in her motor home Jan was finishing up her chores. She had some light soft music on the CD player. A glass of white wine filled her hand. She was smiling. Again she thought of the girl in her singles group that had recommended this beach. It was indeed as beautiful as it had been described. With her wine in one hand and a lawn chair in the other she descended the steps to the sand. In a moment the chair was in a spot where she could see and admire the sea. Brushing the hair from her eyes she sat down.

For the first time she noticed a man by the truck a short distance away. She felt a little wistful. Traveling alone, she missed the camaraderie of another person. Jan had noticed the Chevy truck and camper as she pulled in and parked. It had a Canadian flag flying from the radio antenna so she was pretty sure it belonged to a Canadian couple. She was still a bit nervous about traveling alone even though years had passed without the problems feared by single women travelers.

Just inside the door of her coach she kept a baseball bat in case she needed a defensive weapon. Her army issue pistol was in her bedside drawer back in Canada. She often wished she had it with her. But here in Mexico, illegal import of a firearm meant an automatic thirty-five years in prison.

As the sun slowly set behind the swaying palms Jan noticed the flickering yellow flames of a campfire up the beach. The thought of building one herself was soon dismissed. She was bone-tired after a long day driving. At her last stop in Palenque she had walked and visited the Misol Ha National Park and falls. Tomorrow was another day and she could kill some time gathering rocks and wood for a fire of her own.

Her first inkling of trouble came with the approach of a vehicle. The noise of an engine without a muffler was nearly drowned out by the booming of drums and the wail of a trumpet. The sound of Mexican music grew louder. Suddenly a battered up old pickup truck stopped on the beach in front of Jan's RV. There were two young men in the cab and three more in the box. They were jabbering in Spanish and Jan could only pick up the odd word.

Suddenly the engine noise stopped and the blaring music became silent.

"Hello lady," shouted the driver, leaving the truck. "Donde esta, I mean where is your man Chiquita?"

Jan remained seated, her fear building, even her baseball bat would be useless against five men.

"He's gathering firewood," she replied," He'll be right back."

"Lady you got cervesa, I mean beer for us?" said another, younger man, with a heavy Spanish accent.

"I saw you in Chetumal today." The driver continued, "There was no man! You are alone? Si?"

Suddenly Jan felt cold. She was trapped. This gang of young ruffians had obviously been drinking and knew she was alone and beyond help from anyone. She debated on giving them a case of beer then thought better of it. They were already drunk, and more beer would only make them bolder.

By now they had all left the truck and were circling around her. One of them looked into the coach and saw the open bottle of white wine inside the door.

"Amigos, vino blanco," he exclaimed before tipping the bottle back and guzzling its contents.

It was enough to excite the others as two of them entered the coach and began to search for more wine. Within minutes another bottle was found and opened. Meanwhile another intruder had opened the outside door of a lower storage compartment. There he found two cardboard cases, each containing a dozen cans of beer.

"Eeeeeeyiiiii, Cervesa!" He shouted, tearing open the case and extracting several of the cans.

Within seconds each of her uninvited guests was sucking on a can of Heineken Export, Her favorite European beer.

The driver of the truck, obviously the leader approached Jan with a full can in each hand. "Hey Chiquita, my name is Jose." Then he added seductively, "You have a cervesa with me? Yes?"

Jan swallowed, hoping her eyes did not betray her fear. Even his voice sickened her. "No, thank you,' she replied, avoiding eye contact. Deep inside she knew where this was heading. They were going to take advantage of her To them she was just a defenseless Norte Americano puta .

She was about to be raped. She was helpless and

she knew it. She had been given some advice a long time ago. An instructor had said that the best thing a woman could do while being raped was to not panic. She needed to keep her wits about her, and wait for a chance to escape. She had always considered that a wise action, but right now she wished she had not worn the white two-piece swimsuit.

Her 34C breasts filled out the top and showed far more cleavage than she would normally reveal. But on a deserted beach it was safe. Wasn't it? But then they would probably behave this way no matter what she was wearing.

Jose finished one can of beer and started on the second one. He could not take his eyes off this woman. She was so beautiful, and her dark hair and tan made her look almost Mexican. He wanted to pull her top down, to see her lovely breasts. Were they white or tanned? Did she have nice big nipples or little bumps like his sister?

He smiled at the thought of peeking at his sister when she was taking a bath. Some day he was going to do more than peek at her. But this woman was here, and ripe for him to pick. The others would also want to poke her in turn. The second passenger from the front seat of the old pickup approached Jan.

"Hello missy, I'm Manuel, and I think we should get to know each other better." Leering at her, he thrust his hand under her suit top and clutched her breast.

It happened so fast that Jan hardly had a chance to react. She turned her head and bit Manuel's wrist.

He howled as he yanked back his left hand and slapped her viciously with his right. A third man grabbed her, lifted her from the chair, and pushed her to the ground. The fourth pulled a wicked looking knife from his belt and pointed it at her throat.

Finally betraying her fear, her eyes grew wide as

she watched the blade approach her throat. When she had bought this suit she had admired the sneaky way they had hidden the front catch. It was hard to see but so easy to do up and undo. She now cursed it as Jose grabbed it and the flimsy hooks came undone. In an instant her breasts were exposed. Her traitorous nipples pointed upward, as if denying their innocence to these thugs.

Jose was amazed for a moment at how easy her top had come off, she looked even better than he had imagined. He reached for the bottom part of the swimsuit with both hands, determined to pull it down those lovely legs and expose the rest of the goddess-like body. Jan was rigid with fear. She felt the bottom of her suit moving as Jose grabbed it.

Manuel had stopped squeezing her breasts and was opening his ragged trousers. Another attacker was trying to kiss her. She was trying to struggle out from under them but they had her pinned down. But for the knife at her throat she would have kicked and fought like a wildcat. But relaxing a bit just helped him to remove her tiny, panty-like bottoms.

Jose was on his knees between Jan's legs staring at her neatly trimmed pubic hair. He could not believe his luck. He was actually going to enjoy taking this tourist woman. This goddess had a body like he had never seen before. He reached to undo his thick leather belt.

Jan heard the rasping sound of a zipper being slid down. She looked at Jose. Again she struggled but could not move, she heard more zippers beside her. She knew she was not only going to be gang raped, but possibly killed, or left for dead. Again she felt a hand grab her breast and she instinctively clamped her teeth on the arm. This time she bit hard and deep, a savage growl rose in her throat as she sank her teeth in. She never saw the fist that hit her.

Manuel punched her on the side of her face with

all his strength. Jan saw a flash of light then nothing more. The blow knocked her unconscious.

Chapter Four

Down the beach Hal finished cleaning the fish and carefully filleted it, leaving the skin on. After slashing the flesh crossways he rubbed some onion soup powder into the fillets. While leaving it to marinate he built a fire from dry palm branches and coconut husks. He propped a reflector up beside the fire. As the husks quickly burned down he added a heap of charcoal. The charcoal would provide a more constant heat and the metal reflector would concentrate the heat from the coals to cook the trout. Finally he sprayed the campfire grill with cooking oil. Unknowingly, his reflector had blocked the view of the fire from anyone farther along the beach.

He had eaten the last of the meat he had brought from home and he looked forward to the change. Thinking of the trout marinating in the fridge he opened a can of beer and took a long drink. He could almost taste the fish, cooked to a golden brown and lightly onion flavored. He had been preparing a salad to accompany the fish when he heard the noise of the old truck coming down the beach.

When its one functioning headlight went out and the noise stopped he knew it had stopped at his neighbors RV. In the dying light of sunset Hal had watched the woman, looking to see her husband. None had appeared. He wondered if she were foolish enough to travel alone.

In a moment he could see vague shadows inside the coach. They disappeared and Hal could hear shouts, laughter, and several male voices. Most of their exchange was in Spanish and his limited vocabulary had him wondering what they were saying. Now curious Hal reached into the truck for his high-powered binoculars. He focused them on the distant coach and watched.

His first inkling of trouble was a guy drinking from what looked like a wine bottle. The woman was sitting in the chair in full view when one of the guys grabbed at her breast; a moment later he slapped her.

"Shit!" exclaimed Hal. "Not on my watch!"

He grabbed his dive belt and set off in his limping lope as he strapped it on. Besides the long, razor sharp dive knife it held a heavy steel bar for prying abalone from the rocks. Favoring the artificial left foot he headed up the beach as fast as his still sore muscles would let him.

As he approached the group he realized there were five guys not the two or three he had expected. The woman was on her back in the sand held by three assailants while a fourth guzzled wine from a bottle and the fifth one was between her legs. They had all lowered their zippers and their intent was obvious.

The old truck sat on the sandy beach between Hal and the others. The sun had set but there was still enough light to see clearly. With the sounds the men made laughing and joking combined with the noise of the waves, Hal's approach went undetected. First he checked the truck. He made sure there were no more guys in it. There were no weapons in sight. He made a mental note of the hand-lettered sign on the door.

It read "Jose Menendez, Mariscos, Bahia de Chetumal". So they were local fishermen, out to raise some hell. With the odds at five to one he had to use the element of surprise and make his first attack count. A preemptive strike would be decisive. Circling to the front of the truck Hal pulled the dive knife with his right hand and unhooked the abalone iron with his left.

As he rounded the front of the truck it became obvious that the woman was unconscious. He caught a brief glimpse of her face in his haste, and she looked vaguely familiar. The thought galvanized him into action as he rushed the group. His first target was Jose, the big guy on his knees and about to plunge his rigid member into the girl.

Hal swung the knife crosswise and severed the Achilles tendons on both of Jose's feet. He would be unable to walk for some time. As he finished the knife swing with his right hand he swung the iron in his left. It caught the next closest Mexican just above his right ear. He went down in a slump.

The surprise was beginning to sink in. The closest rapist to Hal raised a nearly empty wine bottle as a weapon. The knife flashed again, coming back tinged with blood as Hal slashed the upper arm. Cut to the bone, the man dropped the bottle to the beach. The fourth man came at Hal swinging the lawn chair.

The sun-bronzed rescuer easily ducked under the chair. He dropped to one knee and hit the assailant low and hard. The heavy steel bar struck bone just under the kneecap.

The man howled and dropped as the last of the attackers shouted, "Vamanos," and headed for the truck. Crawling, staggering, limping, and trailing blood the five would-be rapists fled. They clambered into and onto the old pickup and raced up the jungle trail away from the beach.

Hal found himself breathing desperately hard and shaking uncontrollably. Fearing the worst, he turned to the naked woman on the sand. A large bruise was appearing on her cheekbone but she was breathing. She looked so familiar. Then he recognized her. It was Jan, his nurse from the C-130. Lifting her in his arms he climbed the three short steps into the RV. Despite his best efforts her bare breasts against his chest did not go unnoticed.

There was a bed in the back so Hal laid her there and covered her with a bed sheet. He was gently washing her bruised cheek with a cool cloth when her eyes opened. She pulled back in fright and ready to fight when she realized where she was.

"You're okay. It's okay," said Hal gently. "They're gone!"

The cold look of fright and fear was still in her eyes. "But how did I get here? And who are you?" She tried to sit up. Then realized she was naked as the covers fell away. Hal had another glimpse of her perfect breasts.

"Where are my clothes?" She asked as she quickly covered herself. Hal explained slowly that he had chased off her attackers then carried her inside. Adding that he was her neighbor from down the beach.

"But!" she interrupted. "Did they? I mean was I?" Then the events of the last hour caught up with her and she began to cry. She sobbed uncontrollably so Hal lay down beside her and took her in his arms.

"No!" he said. "I don't think they had time before I came along and stopped them." Hal touched his dive knife and the abalone bar, I had some help though, and it's just too bad I didn't have a gun.

"But there were five of them!" She was incredulous.

Hal just smiled, "No ma'am, just four of them, the last one ran before I got to him."

"But your arm?" she asked, noticing the blood for the first time. "You're bleeding!"

"No, it's not my blood," replied the tall, tanned and nearly nude stranger.

Glancing over his lean, well-conditioned body Jan suddenly realized that this guy was a gorgeous hunk. And he looked so familiar. She'd met him somewhere before. He had muscles in places where most guys his age didn't have places. She couldn't help but notice the outline in his trunks just below where the abdominal ripples disappeared below the blue fabric. For the first time she noticed the ugly red scars on his left side. It looked like he had been in a terrible accident, and not that long ago. Suddenly, it came to her.

"Hal?" she whispered.

"Yeah. I guess we meet again. Too bad it's under these circumstances."

They talked for a while longer and Jan slowly relaxed. She was still in awe of the man's heroic actions. They both knew that they could have been killed had things gone wrong. Hal stood at the end of the bed and spoke softly.

"I want you to stay right there. My truck is just up the beach a little ways and I am going to move it down here. I don't think they'll be back but they won't try anything with another vehicle here. In the morning we we'll go and speak to the police."

Jan looked worried for a moment and Hal asked if she wanted his knife to keep her company.

"No," she replied, "I have help here, if I need it."She pointed to the baseball bat beside the door.

Hal looked at her with a quizzing expression.

"My baseball bat!" How could she ever thank him? She wondered silently. He'd definitely stepped up, as most military and non-military guys would. As any good man would. It had been far too long since she'd had a good man, any man, in her life.

Chapter Five

Hal limped back to the truck, his adrenaline rush was wearing off. He packed up his things, drove down the beach, and parked along side Jan's RV. He approached the coach and knocked on the door. By this time it was getting quite dark.

"Jan," he called, "It's me, Hal."

A light came on inside the rig and Hal could see Jan. She was now fully dressed, sitting in the driver's seat, clasping the baseball bat to her chest. She pressed a button and electrically unlocked the door.

"Come in Hal," she called.

He opened the door and climbed up into the coach. During his earlier trip he hadn't noticed the interior decor. Although an older model, the rig was elegantly decorated and immaculately kept.

Jan was staring through the windshield. There was nothing to see save the luminescent flash as the waves hit the beach. In her one hand was the bat, in the other a glass of red liquid. She noticed Hal looking at her glass and held it aloft for him to see. "It's a bloody Mary," she quipped. "Those rotten bastards drank my wine and most of my beer. Good thing they didn't find the liquor cabinet. At least I have some vodka and some other booze left. You deserve a drink. What can I get you?"

"Nothing, really," replied Hal. "I just wanted to make sure you were alright. I'll be right outside your door, if you need anything, just holler. I'm a light sleeper."

"Like hell," replied the dark haired beauty. "What kind of gentleman would leave a lady to drink all by her lonesome? There's the vodka, some rye whiskey, rum, scotch, and tequila. In the fridge there's canned pop, and clamato juice. Please help yourself. There are glasses over the fridge."

"Okay," he answered, you talked me into it. But only because you are a lady in distress."He opened the cabinet and selected a bottle of Bacardi's, noting that the inside of the cabinet was finished in red velvet with gold piping. Retrieving a glass he poured a generous shot of the white rum and topped it off with coca-cola.

"Schlantzevahr!" he toasted lifting his glass to his lips.

"What the hell was that?" asked Jan, "And what does it mean?"

"It's an old Scottish toast from the highlands. My grandma taught it to me. Roughly translated it means To Your Health!"

"Oh okay," replied Jan, a slight smile appearing below her bruised cheek and black eye. "Then here's to you and up your kilt! And thank you my Scottish friend for my health, my pride, and my life." Her voice cracked as the memories of the previous hours ran through her mind.

Hal remained silent. He had never met a woman quite like her. Not only was she attractive and had a body built for loving, she was smart.

Over the next half hour Jan told him the story about losing her husband and how she had learned to look after things without him. She told Hal about checking the oil, dumping the holding tanks, filling with water, and even checking the pressure in all six of the tires.

Of all the women Hal had known, none of them

had ever appeared with a tire gauge in their hand. Most of them could barely cook let alone do any actual work. He felt a familiar stirring in his trunks as he admired the long dark hair, deep brown eyes, and sumptuous lips. Even after the near rape, with the bruised face, and without makeup she looked better than most women did after a total makeover.

Suddenly Hal felt very tired. After four hours swimming around the reef and the fight he was worn out. He finished his drink and said goodnight.

Jan felt a little disappointed but she was also tired. It had been a long drive and the fight with five men had left her tired, sore, and bruised. Somehow she knew the budding friendship with Hal was just beginning. She had noticed the interest he had taken in checking her out. She wondered if he realized she had also checked him over and admired his package as well.

* * * *

The next morning Hal was awake at sunrise. The sound of crashing waves, birds singing, and the wind whistling through the palm trees welcomed him. He rose and pulled on a pair of cutoff jeans and a dark t-shirt. After brushing his teeth he decided to shave before checking on his shapely neighbor. The day before he had a face full of whiskers after not shaving for a few days. He knew from experience that most women disliked prickly-faced unshaven men.

After breakfasting on coffee and toast he stepped outside and noticed Jan was up and the door of her coach was open. She was busy at the stove.

"Good morning good looking," Hal called, as he approached her door. "You're up early. How are you feeling?"

"I feel great considering the circumstances," replied Jan. "Come on in, the coffee is ready and I was just about to call you. I'll have bacon and eggs ready in just a jiffy."

"You don't need to do that," he replied. Noting that she seemed quite at ease while frying bacon, poaching eggs, and making toast at the same time.

"Nonsense," she answered. "After last night you need a good meal to get your strength back." She almost added that he might need it for a more pleasant reason. For a moment she fantasized him in bed with her but kept the lustful thought to herself. When they had finished eating breakfast and were enjoying their second cup of coffee Hal broke the silence.

"We should really get packed up and head into Chetumal and see the police. I think I know who at least one of them were." He explained the sign on the side of the truck.

"Of course," she replied. "And Mariscos means seafood, specifically shellfish which around here means shrimp."

Hal shook his head in wonderment, "I suppose you speak Spanish as well?" he asked.

"Well enough to get by with," she answered. "I took Spanish in school and I've been practicing since I arrived in Mexico. Anyway, that means at least one of those guys is in the shrimping business."

* * * *

The winding road through the jungle ended in Xcalac. Here they took the gravel road to Santa Rosa, then on to the main highway into Chetumal. Because he was more familiar with the route Hal led the way in the old camper truck.

Jan followed close behind, afraid of losing sight of him in the traffic. There seemed to be no end to the rickety old trucks loaded down with sugar cane headed for the mills in Belize.

They found a spot to park near the Estacion de

Policia in downtown Chetumal. With Jan's knowledge of Spanish and the fact that the chief of police spoke some English they were able to report the attack and subsequent fight.

Hal wrote down the name from the side of the truck for him. Jan explained that they must be shrimpers from Chetumal.

After listening to their story the officer excused himself and made a phone call. A moment later he handed the instrument to Hal. A voice on the other end introduced a woman speaking perfect English.

She asked Hal to explain what had happened. After listening for several minutes she asked to speak to the Chief again. What followed was an exchange in rapid fire Spanish that neither of the Canadian tourists could understand. As the conversation ended the heavyset policeman hung up the phone. He barked an order in Spanish to another officer in an adjoining room. Then he turned to Jan and Hal and spoke in heavily accented English.

"A moment, por favor." Soon the outer door to his office opened and another officer entered pushing a wheelchair. In the chair was a scruffily dressed, unshaven Mexican. Both feet were heavily bandaged and showed signs of seeping blood. He had a grin on his face until he saw the two Canadians. His eyes grew wide and his chin dropped.

The cop pushing the chair spoke with the expected Spanish accent. "Do you know this man?" he asked. "You have seen him before?"

Hal rose from his chair as though expecting a fight. "Yeah!" he shouted. "I cut his feet last night on the beach."

Jan took a moment to recover the shock of seeing his face again. "Yes," she replied. "That bastard tried to rape me."

Most of the day was spent with translators doing

interviews and artists sketching faces. Finally by mid-afternoon they were asked to sign reports and told they could leave. One of the translators came to say farewell and shake their hands.

"They will be punished," he said. "From your description the other four were crew members of the same shrimp boat. Even now they are being arrested."

On the way back to the parked vehicles they passed a small panaderia. Hal took Jan's hand and led her into the tiny Mexican bakery where he bought some hard rolls and soft taco shells.

"How would you like to go back to the beach?" he asked. "But in a different spot."

Jan thought about it for a moment a then nodded her head and smiled. "As long as you park right beside me."

Hal saw the little smile and wondered what he had done to please the Gods so much that they sent her to him. "Have you ever tried snorkeling?" Hal asked as they reached the parking lot.

"No," replied Jan. "But I would like to try it if you're the teacher."

Chapter Six

While returning to the coast Hal wondered where he could rent some SCUBA gear. If he could get Jan interested in snorkeling maybe he could teach her how to dive with an air tank. There were so many places they could explore. Maybe the diving gods heard his thoughts when he wished he had someone to share the scenic depths with. The only problem with deeper diving was finding a reputable spot to get the tanks refilled with good clean air. They might have to go north to Playa del Carman or perhaps even Cancun to get equipment. Hal hated the thought of going to the larger city. Cancun was more like New York than a Mexican resort. But if they had to go that far he would take her to the island. Isla Mujeres had some great reefs for novice divers. It would make a great classroom for Jan.

The sun had almost set by the time they pulled onto the isolated beach near Ziquipal. It was a long way from their previous spot. But here on the shore of Bahia de la Acension they could enjoy the beach, the reef, and the calmer sea in the protected waters of the bay. They would have arrived sooner but they had problems finding a store where they could get Jan a mask, a snorkel, and a pair of fins. She also wanted a one-piece suit to replace the white one she had been wearing. Hal rebelled slightly, preferring to see her in a bikini, but she stood her ground.

While Jan got her rig set up and mixed them each a drink Hal dug a fire pit and lit a fire. He congratulated himself for putting the trout in the fridge to marinate before Jan's attackers arrived. Jan came out with the drinks and set up two lawn chairs. Hal was busy on his outside fold-down table.

"Do you think you could give me a hand?" he asked, handing her a knife. "Start slicing, please." First he sliced some fresh lettuce and put it in a bowl and covered it.

Her knife made short work of a large red onion, leaving it in thin rings. Finally he sliced up a plump red tomato. From the fridge he brought a bottle of salsa and a jar of guacamole.

"I think the fire is ready." The coals were perfect in the fire pit. He set up the reflector and placed the grill over the fire then placed the fillets on the grill. While they were cooking Hal retrieved the fresh tacos from the cab of his truck.

"I hope you like fish tacos," he said.

Her face became a mask of curiosity as she watched what he was doing. "I don't think I have ever had one," she answered. "How do you make them?"

"Well watch and learn," he suggested. He let the fish cook skin side down for several minutes then flipped them over. Next he spread the tacos wide open. "Okay now you put some lettuce on one side."

As directed she placed a layer of chopped lettuce on the taco. On the other side he spread some sliced onion and tomato.

"Now put some salsa and a gob of guacamole on the lettuce and we're nearly done." Taking a beat up old spatula he lifted the trout pieces from the grill and placed them on the table, skin side up. "Now we need to skin the fish, it's really simple, do it like this."

Working carefully with his dive knife he peeled off the skins and placed a half of a steaming trout fillet on the lettuce. Jan did the same, her piece of trout's skin also peeled off easily.

"Now the piece de resistance." He took a shaker of spice from inside the door. After sprinkling a tiny amount of Chipotle chili powder on them he folded the tacos over. "Fish taco with fresh sea trout for the lady," he proclaimed, handing one of his creations to Jan.

She took a small bite and began to chew, almost as if she were experimenting. In a moment she was smiling. "This is delicious," she mumbled through a mouthful of fish and lettuce. She swallowed before continuing, "So you can cook, too!"

Hal grinned, "Well I like to cook sometimes. Restaurant food gets so boring and you never really get quite what you want." He bit into his own taco and they both ate in silence. As he finished his taco he quickly made two more from the remaining fillet. Jan willingly accepted the second helping.

"But where did you get the fish?" she asked.

"Yesterday, while snorkeling on the reef, I got it with my spear gun.

"Well you certainly are a man of many talents." She stated, wondering to herself if he was that talented in bed. Hal cleaned up the table and washed the few utensils he had used. The stump of his leg was aching and the prosthetic foot was beginning to chafe the scarred tissue. He really wanted to go for a swim but he felt a need to pay more attention to Jan. His feelings for her were deepening since the rescue. He was afraid to scare her off or offend her. He decided to just be friendly and let her make the next move.

"So," he said. "Let's get you fitted with this snorkel gear. Tomorrow I want to show you what life on the reef is like but first you have to learn a few things." Using his own mask he showed her how to spit in the inside of the glass and rub it around then rinse it off. She looked puzzled until he explained that the spit would stop the inside of the glass from fogging up in the water. He adjusted the strap and showed her how to don the mask. Next he had her try the mouthpiece of the snorkel and try breathing through it. She found it wasn't quite as simple as it seemed. He attached the snorkel to the strap on her face-mask.

"You have to remember that if your head goes under water the open end of the snorkel will flood. You have to hold your breath until it is up again and then blow the water out so you can breathe. We'll practice in the shallow water after breakfast."

The black and blue bruise on Jan's face was beginning to fade to a bluish green. It was still quite tender but under the circumstances she felt lucky that was her only wound. She wondered about his wounds. They looked much better than what she had seen on the plane. She decided she would watch him closely. An infection here in the jungle could turn serious quickly.

That evening they sat by the campfire and watched the waves crashing onto the beach. The white crests of the waves glowed with a strange greenish light. Microorganisms in the water gave off phosphorescence when agitated. For hundreds of yards into the bay, and up and down the beach, these unique creatures illuminated the waves.

Overhead the moonless sky revealed millions of stars in the full, black, and endless expanse of the heavens. Sparks from the fire drifted slowly upward before extinguishing. From the jungle behind them came the night sounds: cicadas, night birds, and the screech of howler monkeys frolicking in the treetops. The beach and the water here was similar to their earlier spot. There were more palms, the jungle was closer and denser, and there were no trails through the trees.

For a long time neither of them spoke, each absorbed in the tranquil setting of this place. Finally it was Hal that broke the silence.

"Would you mind terribly if I took this phony foot

off? It is really beginning to bother me."

"Sure, go ahead," replied Jan, seeing her chance. "But how is it? Probably sore at times, but no infections?" Hal took a swallow of his beer, gazing out to sea; a blank look came over his face. He knew the question was coming. But he never seemed to get over the chill that surrounded him when it came. The moment that he could not remember haunted him with the damage he had received.

"It's fine, and the same with these," he said holding up the mutilated left hand. "The side of my leg hurts and the ribs haven't healed yet. My hearing will probably never be the same."

"Oh my God!" exclaimed Jan, "I am so sorry."

"It's okay, I'm getting used to it. The foot and I get along OK, it is the rest of me that got really beat up. I do miss the fingers though." Jan reached across and put her hand on his forearm.

"All those scars, it is a wonder you weren't killed." "Yup," came the response. "Thanks to the guys in my section, a nearby helicopter, and some super medics in the field hospital! I don't remember much; I never knew what hit me until I woke two days later. I got lucky, a lot of friends didn't make it home alive."

"Hal, believe me, I understand. I was there. I was the triage nurse when your team brought you in with the Nyala. And yes we didn't think you would make it. My husband didn't! I lost him to a mine near Kandahar." She lied. " I still miss him so much. Such a wonderful man, such a waste." She was beginning to feel guilty telling Hal this wild story.

He turned to look at her, her face showed the hurt. She knew! He met so few people that really did understand. She had seen the results of the IEDs used by the insurgents. The Improvised Explosive Device had become a favored weapon among the Taliban. They would pile several obsolete high explosive artillery shells in a shallow hole beside a road. A hidden observer would activate it when an allied vehicle drove by. Simply dialing the number of a cellular phone rigged in the package detonated it. Even the LAV III Light Armoured Vehicle was no match for these deadly mine-like packages of death.

In one horrific split second men were turned from healthy young soldiers to quivering masses of blood soaked flesh, dead in an instant.

Hal put his hand on hers and looked into her eyes. A tiny tear hung there. Even though she chose to lie about it she would never forget how her first love had been. They sat in silence for many minutes before Hal reconnected his foot to the stump.

"Well lady, if you will excuse me, nature is calling, and then I am going to bed. I'll see you in the morning for diving lessons."

"Goodnight Hal, thank you again, and I do understand." As she climbed into the coach she realized her attraction to the man with the artificial foot had become even stronger during the past few hours.

Chapter Seven

As the dawn broke on another beautiful day Hal sniffed the air from the comfort of his bed. Coffee! That gorgeous creature next door was doing it again. He spent a few minutes attaching his foot, donning shorts and shirt, and brushing his teeth. As he opened the camper door Jan called to him.

"Coffee is ready if you are, Hal!" It took only a moment to traverse the space between their RVs. Hal was climbing the three steps as he replied.

"Yup, and so am I. Good morning. I hope you had a good sleep, and you're ready to go diving?"

"Yes," she announced. "As soon as I finish my coffee and get my new bathing suit on."

Hal tried not to stare at her. To him she was the most beautiful woman in the world. Her hair was pulled up in a ponytail; she wore no makeup or jewelry. On her left ring finger was a light colored indent where she had once worn a ring.

By the time they finished breakfast and got outside to organize their day the sun was well up and it was getting warmer. The sea was almost flat calm, a perfect day for snorkeling. In the jungle the daily ruckus had begun. The voices of howler monkeys joined the calls of dozens of bird species as they flitted from tree to tree seeking their breakfast.

Hal had all their equipment out. He was ready to head for the water when Jan stepped out of her rig. It was his first view of her new bathing suit and for a moment he was awe-struck. She had looked good as he carried her indoors after the attack. She now looked like a candidate for a Miss America Pageant.

It was nothing fancy, just a plain, light blue, no frills one piece suit but it made her look like a goddess. Jan saw the look on his face and smiled.

"You like?" she asked, a teasing musical lilt to her voice as she turned playfully in a circle.

"Um, yeah, wow!" stammered Hal, "Great outfit, you just keep looking better all the time." His physical reaction to her appearance was not wasted on Jan and she smiled even more when he turned away in an attempt to hide his body's very masculine response.

"So let's get wet!" he called over his shoulder. The next half hour was spent showing Jan the intricacies of snorkel diving. At first he had her practice in shallow water. It took her a few tries. She came up choking on seawater more than once. But she finally learned the trick to the snorkel.

When she lowered her head to look under or behind the snorkel would flood. It gave her a mouthful of water every time. Hal taught her how to take a breath and hold it while her head was under water. Then to use that air to blow the water out of the plastic tube so she could breathe again.

She was an avid swimmer so the fins on her feet came naturally. The hardest part was learning how to drain water from her mask. She had to hold one side against her face and blow out through her nose to drive the water out.

Suddenly she felt Hal take her hand. He pointed seaward and she nodded. She forgot the snorkel. When it flooded she surfaced gasping and choking.

Minutes later they were slowly cruising toward a nearby reef. Jan was amazed by the clarity of the water. On the light brown sandy bottom lay thousands of seashells, remnants of shellfish from days gone by.

She saw several sand dollars and would have liked to retrieve them except it meant diving to the bottom. She was not yet that comfortable with the snorkel.

Hal kept checking her to make sure she was okay until she seemed more relaxed. He began to point out items of interest. The sandy bottom was rippled with row upon row of tiny ridges, formed by the action of the waves.

In many places she saw single ridges going in a different direction. By following this trail in the sand she would find a snail like creature moving slowly across the bottom.

Even on this remote beach there were signs of human habitation. Civilization brought the inevitable pollution. She saw assorted bottles, old tires, and bits of rope attached to old fishing nets. There were rusting pieces of iron and steel protruding from the coral. As the water grew deeper the color changed. Toward the bottom it became blue as the sea filtered out the sunlight.

She soon saw the first of the sea fans. Their stems anchored to the bottom and the large round leaves waving gently. As they approached the reef the first of the fish population became evident. Singly, in pairs, or in schools numbering hundreds of individuals, they flashed in the sun. Jan stopped swimming. There was so much to see. She hung motionless in the water taking in the beauty below her. Hal noticed that he had left her behind and quickly returned.

Using the agreed upon signals he held out his hand with thumb and forefinger in the circular shape meaning Okay? Jan returned the sign and lifted her head from the water. She removed the snorkel mouthpiece from her mouth as Hal's head appeared.

"This is unbelievable!" She gasped. "I never would have imagined it!"

Hal smiled, admiring the incredulous expression on her face. "I thought you would enjoy it," he quipped. "Can you see now why I wanted to be a professional diver? It is a great place to work. Well, most of the time anyway. Hey I have to show you something, wait here. I'll be right back."

With that Hal put the snorkel back in and performed an effortlessly executed surface dive. As he bent at the waist and pointed his head down his arms made one powerful breaststroke. At the same time he straightened out, forcing his legs, good and artificial, straight up into the air. As his legs came out of the water their weight helped drive him down in a graceful descent. A second later he was kicking gently, heading for the bottom. He chose a nearby sea fan and cut it off with the ever-present dive knife. Jan watched his dive and the ascent back to her side. They both resumed snorkel breathing as he showed her the fan under water.

He pointed to several brown lumps nearly perfectly camouflaged to the color of the leaf. She looked at him for a moment, wondering what he wanted her to see. Was she missing something?

Hal held up one finger, meaning "just a moment" then gently touched one of the brown blobs. The transformation was as amazing as it was nearly instantaneous. The brown coloring was a very thin mantle covering a living creature. As the veil-like membrane retracted it exposed a beautiful pink and white cowry. The shell was the size of her thumb. Hal picked it off and handed it to her. It was very smooth, hard and shiny.

She had often seen jewelry, necklaces, and earrings made of cowry shells but had no idea where they came from. Hal pulled a small net bag from under his suit. He dropped the shell into the bag and picked off the remaining three creatures, adding them to the bag and attaching it to his belt.

They resumed cruising the reef. For over an hour Hal pointed out various creatures living among the coral. She felt like she was in a huge aquarium. There were lobsters and crabs, moray eels, stingrays, groupers, and more. Jan nearly swallowed her snorkel in surprise and fright when Hal pointed out a shark cruising the edge of the reef. Her first thought was a scene from the movie "Jaws".

After an hour Hal turned them around and headed toward the beach. Jan could have stayed out all day and never tired of seeing the wonders of the sea. As Hal swam beside her she reached over and took his hand. He gently squeezed it in response.

Forgetting the snorkel by her left ear Jan turned her head to the right to smile and nod at Hal. The greeting exploded in a fit of coughing. She choked as the snorkel submerged and she sucked in a mouthful of salt water.

Hal shook his head and laughed, spitting out the black rubber mouthpiece. "Damned wannabes," he chortled. "Can't hardly find a real diver anymore!"

Slowly Jan got her breathing under control. "Remember, this was your bright idea," she countered. After swimming to the beach together, they were soon toweling off. The breeze was quite cool on their skin after the warmth of the sea. Hal noticed the coolness caused points to appear on her suit as her nipples reacted to the air. He turned away, knowing she would be embarrassed if she knew what he had seen.

Jan shook out her ponytail and rubbed it with the towel. "I wish I had a waterproof camera," she said. "It is so fantastic. Folks will never believe or understand what it's like down there."

Hal sat on a lawn chair in the shade of a coconut palm and removed his swim fin and lower leg. The slightest bit of sand between the prosthesis and his stump created an irritating and aggravating soreness.

"Well hey, I have a camera." He responded. "You're welcome to use it. I guess I forgot what it was like when I first started diving. The wonder kind of wears off and you start taking it for granted. Then someone like you comes along and I see things I've been ignoring for years. I would love to get you certified for SCUBA and take you deeper. This reef is just the beginning. Pardon the pun, but you have only scratched the surface.

"Okay, so what is SCUBA?"Jan clearly had never heard of it.

Hal smiled, "It stands for Self Contained Underwater Breathing Apparatus," he explained. "You must have seen pictures of divers with an air tank on their back? "

"Yes," she said nodding her head. "So how and where do I get this training, and how much does all that stuff cost?" It wasn't only her new-found interest in diving that Jan was thinking of. It was another way to get to know Hal better. She was realizing she wanted to share his interests. Most of all she wanted to spend more time with this wonderful hunk of male excellence.

Chapter Eight

Before he went to bed Hal had retrieved the four cowries from his dive bag and cleaned them. The first task was to get the snail-like creatures out of the shells. In order to do that, unfortunately, they first had to be killed. He did this as humanely as he could by submersing them in straight alcohol. Next he put them in a jar of fresh water and set them in the sun. The dead but rubbery occupants softened overnight. Early the next morning, before Jan was up, he took out a small air compressor and a fine nozzle. With a blast of air he blew the little bodies out of their shells.

Next he used a small high-speed drill and a diamond rasp to drill a hole in the end of each stone-like shell. Hal had done this many times when he was short of cash. He carried the necessary fittings to make jewelry to sell to tourists.

Jan was preparing breakfast and finally grew curious as to what Hal was doing so when she ventured over to his camper. She looked in through the screen door just as Hal completed assembling the second of a pair of earrings. "And might I ask what you are so busy at?"

Hal opened the door and asked her in. Once she was seated at the table beside him he took her hand and deposited his handiwork in her palm. "For you," he said, watching for her response.

Jan gasped as she realized what they were, and where they had come from. "From the reef?" She queried. "From our first dive?

"That's them," he answered. "I Just cleaned them up a little bit. I thought you would like something to remember your first trip to a reef."

Jan felt a lump in her throat and felt the tears coming. She never dreamed those little shells could make anything so beautiful. Nor could she imagine this rough and ready male warrior having the skill and patience to create jewelry. She turned to face him. On impulse, not knowing what to say, she kissed him. A brief gentle touch of lips at first until his arms went around her. Then the hidden feelings they had each suppressed for the past few days were unleashed. She felt Hal's tongue gently explore her lips and she responded by touching his with hers. When they finally separated she felt light-headed and shaky. She looked into his gentle brown eyes.

"Thank you," she offered. "That is the most wonderful gift I have ever received." She held the dangling shells by the gold loops and admired them in the sunlight. "Do you have a mirror?" She asked, reaching to attach the gold fittings to her pierced ear lobes.

"Right behind you," answered Hal. "They sure look great against your tan."

Jan turned and looked at her reflection, moving her head side to side. "They're so perfect," she announced. "How can I ever repay you for all you've done?"

Hal stroked his chin as though deep in thought. "Well, how about having dinner with me this evening?"

For the second time in a week she felt the buzz in her belly. She wondered if he would kiss her again. "I should be taking you out to dinner. These are beautiful. Thank you very much."

Hal sat back, totally satisfied with his creations. She was just beaming as she looked into his eyes.

Stunning and radiant were mere words that could not accurately describe her. "You're so welcome Jan!If you want we can collect more and make you a necklace." He smiled as he thought of the kiss he might get for a necklace.

"Really?" she gasped. "But we need to make one for you so we'll have a matching set."

Hal held up both hands in mocking defense in front of him. "Whoa!" he laughed. "I don't wear earrings!

"Well no, I meant just a necklace, maybe one shell on a nice fine gold chain. It would look so good on you.

"You' ll have to learn how to surface dive and get to the bottom," teased the veteran diver. "If I am going to wear a necklace, you have to collect the cowry. Meanwhile come on, we have some other collecting to do."

Jan began to gather her diving gear but Hal said, "No, we are going *that* way." He pointed toward the jungle. From a compartment on the camper he retrieved a burlap sack and a long steel machete. Jan looked on in wonderment. What was he going to do now? Hal led the way through the coconut palms, on the ground lay dozens, maybe hundreds of coconuts in various stages of decay. Finally he picked up a green specimen. "This is what we want," he said, hefting the huge nut and giving it a shake before dropping it into the sack. "We need a half dozen or so."

They continued deeper into the jungle; Hal was obviously looking for something. They had walked for just a few minutes when he stopped. He took the razor sharp machete from the scabbard on his belt. Jan couldn't help but look around. The noise from the birds was almost deafening. They flitted from tree to tree, seemingly upset by the presence of these strangers. Suddenly she saw a larger shape fly from one tree to the next.

"Oh! Look!" she exclaimed, as the howler monkey added its voice to the cacophony of jungle sounds.

Hal had stopped near a large bush-like tree; its leaves were huge, perhaps six feet long and two feet wide. It reminded her of the trees in a banana plantation she and Dick had once visited. From the ground a tangle of long thin vines wound upward to the top of the tree. Hal grasped one and began to pull it down. Breaking off a piece several feet long he handed it to his staring companion. She took the vine and looked in wonder. Spaced along the slender branch were several blossoms. They appeared to be roses except they were brown, dry, and woody.

"Wood roses." explained Hal. "These jungles are full of them.

"They are exquisite," she replied in astonishment. "I've never seen anything like them." Meanwhile, with a few swings of the machete, Hal had cleared away the older lower leaves exposing the newer growth. In a moment six of the giant green leaves were on the ground.

"Can you handle this?" he asked, handing Jan the sack of coconuts. He returned the machete to his belt. With both arms he scooped up the fresh leaves and headed back toward the beach. Jan had absolutely no idea what any of it was for.She would know before this day was done. This amazing man was going to surprise her again, not once but twice. She somehow knew she was going to be kissing him again before the night was over.

Chapter Nine

Back on the beach Hal began to dig a hole in the sand. Jan watched, wondering what this guy would do next. He had amazed her so many times already. She had never met anyone like him and she was starting to like the feeling. When the hole was to his liking Hal threw in a bunch of dry coconut husks, the dried stems of big palm leaves and some chunks of wood. After setting fire to the pile he turned to Jan.

"Get your gear. We're going for a short swim."

She responded mechanically, still wondering what was happening but she was ready in just a few moments. Together they crossed the sand to the beach. Jan noticed that he was carrying a net bag and his spear gun. Wading in until the water was knee deep they donned their snorkel gear. Hal led the way to the reef.

As they arrived Hal suddenly arced downward to the edge of a coral outcrop. She watched in wonder as he brought up the spear gun and fired. The long metal shaft shot forward and instantly impaled an unsuspecting lobster. He returned to the surface and held it up for her to see then pulled the spear out and put the creature in the net bag. She followed as he swam along the reef. Hal turned and touched her on the shoulder. When she responded he pointed behind her.

As she turned she almost screamed in fright. Just a few feet away were three large, black, triangular fins protruding from the water. For the second time in a week she visualized a scene from the movie "Jaws." The fins were approaching the floating couple. Jan's face paled as the three long black shapes circled. She had never been this close to anything wild before. She spit out her snorkel.

"Will they bite?" she whispered, her voice trembling with fear.

"No, they won't hurt you," came the reassuring reply. They're dolphins, not sharks. They're friendly. They just stopped to say hello."

Jan smiled weakly, but the relief showed. The dolphins circled once more then slowly continued on their way. Hal and Jan went back to their hunt. They hadn't gone far when again he angled down toward the bottom.

Once more the spear flashed and again he surfaced. This time with a large fish impaled on the barbs. With the fish in the bag they set off once more. Before long the third dive was executed and produced a second lobster. This one was even larger than the first. As the lobster joined the rest of his catch he spit out the mouthpiece.

"Well that's our dinner," he announced, a boyish grin on his face." I hope you like seafood."

Jan mumbled a reply, forgetting the snorkel was still in her mouth. So she nodded her head. As they swam shoreward she looked at the waving sea fans on the bottom. Knowing now what the little brown lumps were, she knew she would be back to gather more of them.

On the beach the fire had burned down so Hal added more wood. Taking the net bag to his outdoor table he first quickly cleaned the fish.

Jan watched with interest. "What kind is it?" she asked.

"It's a sea bass. Not very big as bass go, maybe six pounds, but a nice eating size." Next he opened the bellies of the lobsters and removed the insides. With the catch prepared he reached into the camper and brought out a large bowl. It held an assortment of local fruit and vegetables.

"Would you like a beer? Jan asked, feeling rather useless just standing there watching.

"Sure," he replied. "On TV the chef always has a glass of wine or something while he works."

Moments later Jan reappeared with two cans of beer and a lawn chair. She opened a can and handed it to Hal before opening hers and settling in the chair. She sat back and gazed around.

The azure waves turned to white foam as they rode up on the sand. Overhead the palms swayed and whispered in the wind. Occasionally she caught the smell of wood smoke from the hole in the sand. She watched the tiny sand crabs scurry across the beach. Their feet left a telltale trail as they darted about in a sidewise crab crawl. Off to the left she noticed a different set of tracks; larger, and with a groove, like something was being dragged.

"Hal, what would make those tracks?" she pointed to the trail.

"An Iguana. There are lots of those lizards in Mexico. They come out to hunt on the beach."

Jan seemed contented with his response so he went back to work. The ever-present dive knife was wiped clean of the gore from the fish and now sliced an onion. Next came a lemon, sliced and added to the bowl. Then several stalks of celery were cut up. Jan wondered at the ease with which he worked. It was obviously not his first time in a kitchen. He picked up one of the big leaves from the jungle and chopped off a large piece. This he put on the table and place the gutted fish on it. Next he retrieved one of the green coconuts. Holding it against a log he raised the big machete and swung it down. A piece of the husk flew into the sand. Several more times the blow was repeated until the nut was exposed. Placing it aside he repeated the process with the remaining three nuts.

He turned to Jan. "Would you be so kind as to put three of these in the fridge?" he asked

Jan rose to obey, now more mystified than ever. Back at the table Hal mixed an assortment of sliced fruit and vegetables in a bowl. To them he added dill weed, pepper, salt, and Chipotle powder. He used the point of the dive knife to cut a hole in the end of a coconut. Next he sprinkled the milky white juice onto the mixture. Using his hands he mixed the coconut milk and spices into the contents of the bowl. The strange mixture was then stuffed into the fish's cavity. When it was full he took the sliced lemon and squeezed the juice over the entire fish. Then, holding everything together with one hand he used the other to roll the big green leaf around the fish. A second, larger piece of leaf followed and the bundle was set aside. A similar process followed with each of the lobsters. Over the top of each went a squeeze of lemon, a chunk of butter, and a drizzle of coconut juice. Then they too were wrapped in the giant leaves.

Hal approached the pit where a bed of glowing coals awaited. He gathered an armload of damp seaweed from the beach. This went in on top of the embers. Next he arranged a layer of palm leaves. The bundles of fish and lobster went in, covered with more palm leaves. By now the hole was nearly full and already beginning to steam. A final armload of seaweed was covered with several inches of sand.

"There!" he stated. "A Mexican pit barbecue, luau style. Now I need another beer!"

Jan was amazed. She hoped the taste would be as good as it looked. For the next hour the tantalizing aromas emanating from the pit assured Jan that this dinner would taste divine. Speaking of divine, she glanced over at Hal and smiled. She wouldn't mind nibbling on the chef tonight, as well.

Chapter Ten

Hal watched the changing clouds while sipping his beer. The darkening skies looked like it could rain later, and he hoped it would hold off.

His new-found diving buddy noticed the concern on his face. "Is something wrong?" she asked.

"No, not really, just watching the weather. There could be a storm coming in from the southeast. It might be smart if we put things away and batten the hatches tonight." He busied himself with preparing paper plates and plastic utensils. "I hope you don't mind if I use my best tableware for dinner?"

Jan laughed, she too often used disposables to conserve water and avoid doing dishes. "In fact I have a very nice white wine I have been saving for something special. I think this is about as special as it gets." She got up and walked to her coach.

Hal smiled, wondering if he still had the plastic wine glasses in the camper.

She was soon back, clutching a bottle of wine. I can't pronounce the name but it tastes good," she said." And that's what counts."

Hal accepted the bottle as she handed it over. "Hmm, it is pronounced Gewurztraminer a nice fruity wine, similar to the famous Mosels of Germany."

Jan's chin dropped. "You are a wine expert too? When did you ever get time to learn to swim? But hey, seriously," she continued, "and not to change the subject but I have to know. Do you mind if I ask if you are married?"

Hal shook his head. "Nope! I was but it didn't work out. We were divorced seven years ago. "

"Any kids?" she added. "Again, nope!" came his response. "An old eligible bachelor and getting older."

"You aren't that old," she offered. "And neither am I!

"Okay, I am going to guess that you are thirty-two. That means I am five years older than you are.

"Okay, you're close but I am thirty-three so you are only four years older.

"My turn, do you have any kids?" he asked "No, I had a baby boy but he was stillborn. A heart defect they said.

"Sorry!" he offered in a whisper. Hal checked his watch then went over and touched the sand above the cooking pit. It was still quite hot. Retrieving a shovel from the back of his truck he began to gently remove the layer of sand. As he worked the aroma grew in volume and strength and the steam rose around him. Scooping the seaweed off in a layer, he exposed the green bundles. Trying not to get sand on them he lifted them onto a platter.

"If you want to open that wine, dinner is about ready," he called. Jan opened the screw-cap bottle and poured each of them a plastic goblet of Gewurztraminer. Meanwhile, Hal had brought the platter over and gingerly unwrapped the outside layers. "Damn, that's hot!" he cursed, as he placed one of the lobsters on Jan's plate. With the second crustacean on his own plate be began to unwrap the fish. When it was fully exposed he slid his knife down along the dorsal fin. The entire side of the fish came away from the bones. Next he removed the entire bone structure in one piece, leaving the stuffing behind. After separating a large piece from the skin he placed it on Jan's plate then repeated the process for himself.

Jan tasted a small morsel of fish. "My God!" she exclaimed. "This is wonderful. I have never had better fish." She slowly consumed the flaky white meat. The lemon and dill flavor was just perfect.

"Oops. I almost forgot." Hal rushed into the camper and returned with a small aluminum pot with an amber liquid in it. "Can't eat lobster without drawn butter." He was wearing his boyish grin again. They unwrapped the lobsters. Their shells now changed from green and brown to a bright pink. Jan watched as he broke off the tail. He had previously slit the lower shells and now the large piece of tail meat simply pulled out. Eating with his fingers he dipped the juicy white meat in the butter and took a bite.

Jan tried to copy his action but grimaced when the lobster juice ran down her arm. He dabbed at her with a paper towel then pointed to the sea saying, "We have an ocean full of warm water to bathe in later. Just enjoy. We don't even have to do dishes or wash the floor." They continued to eat in silence, stopping now and then for a sip of wine. He showed her how to crack the claws open and get the meat within. They tried some of the vegetable stuffing and each nodded in approval. Jan had never before eaten a meal where every morsel was as good as or better than the one before.

"Wow, you should open a restaurant."

"I'm just glad you enjoyed it. I don't get to do it very often." A sudden gust of wind blew the paper plates from the table. Hal looked toward the sea. In the distance large black clouds were gathering. The wind grew cold. Hal knew from experience that was the usually the precursor of an approaching hail storm. He began to gather their gear and put it away. Jan took the lawn chairs back to her rig. When she returned he could see a frightened look on her face. It reminded him of rabbit cornered by a fox.

"Jan?" he asked. "What's wrong?

"The clouds," she replied. "I can't stand storms; they scare me to death."

"Then you go inside," ordered Hal. "Draw the curtains and put some music on, you'll be fine." "Will you come with me?" she asked. "Stay with me, please?

"No problem. I'll be there as soon as I get my stuff secure."

The sun had set and the darkening clouds made the approaching storm look even worse. Jan had no sooner drawn the curtains than a blinding flash announced the first bolt of lightning. Seconds later it was followed by the booming thunder. The wind increased quickly and her coach began to shake. The first drops of rain hammered on the roof as the door opened and Hal entered. Soon they could hear the waves pounding on the beach, as the surf rose higher. Hal sat in the easy chair by the door. From all the signs this promised to be a pretty severe storm but here in the tropics they usually didn't last long. Another flash of lightning lit up the coach, followed by thunder. Closer this time! A palm leaf, blown from a nearby tree landed on the roof. Jan jumped, her eyes wide in fear. She was sitting on the couch, her knees drawn up with her arms locked around them. She was trembling, rocking back and forth like a frightened child. Hal moved to the couch and put his arm around her. She nestled beside him, taking strength from his presence. He lifted her chin with a finger and looked into her tear-filled eyes.

"It's okay Jan, everything is fine, and this storm will soon be over." He bent to kiss the wetness of her cheek but she turned her head. Their lips met. His touch melted her fear as she responded. Hal felt it as their embrace continued. It was as if all the fears and anxieties of the past few days just melted away. As the kiss ended he hugged her close and stroked her hair. She tucked her head under his chin.

Before long the rain stopped and the wind diminished. It had been nearly an hour since the last lightning flash and accompanying thunder.

Jan's breathing was slow and deep. He realized she was asleep. Standing up, he lifted her. Gently, as though she were a child, he carried her in and put her on the bed. After pulling the covers over her he lay down beside her. Even with the bedding separating them she snuggled up behind him. He fell asleep with her arm around him while he listened to her breathe. It had been a long time, too long, since he had last shared a bed with a woman.

Chapter Eleven

The day dawned bright and clear. The sun warmed Hal's back as he sat cross-legged on the beach. He held a cup of coffee in his hand. With no surf, there was barely a murmur from the water's edge. Catching the morning sun, tiny wavelets made twinkling sparkles across the bay. Today was the day that Hal had to go to town. He needed groceries, water, propane and to dump the holding tanks.

"Good morning." Jan offered as approached him from behind. She was dressed in a pair of tan slacks and a green top. Wearing her ponytail and pink lipstick, she looked about sixteen. He'd been deep in thought; he was considering his injuries and how they might affect Jan. She may not wish to be attached to a cripple. His wounds were not pretty and he was becoming more self-conscious of his appearance. Besides, it was nearly time for him to return to the hospital. Yet he didn't want to leave Jan alone on the beach.

He had first come to this area to be alone, where his scars were not on public display. Although healing nicely, his mutilated body was far from attractive and would always be scarred. Standing nearby, Jan wondered what was on his mind so early in the morning. In her rig she had been writing in her diary. She was curious how she and Hal would continue to relate. She had very deep feelings for him but she was not sure how he felt about her. She had asked herself if she would feel this way had he not driven off her attackers. Was she attracted to the man, or indebted to his actions, or feeling pity for his battle injuries?

Hal broke the silence, "I have to go to town today," he said. "Will you be okay here?"

His question took her by surprise. They had been together so much the past few days that she hadn't considered the possibility that he might leave her alone on the beach. A sinking feeling began to permeate her brain.

"Hal we have to talk," she replied.

"What is there to talk about? Came his response.

"Where are we going from here?" she asked, confused about her feelings. "You barely know me and I only just know you!" Again her feelings were confused. "Is this just going to end here on the beach? Or do we want it to continue?" Her eyes moistened as the tears began to form.

Hal looked up at her, and saw the concern on her face. He realized they were thinking the same thoughts and it bothered him deeply. He knew they had to discuss it and get everything into the open.

"You know Jan, that I can't even remember your last name. We know nothing about each other except you are a widow and I am wreck. I'll never be whole again. I'm not sure I'm looking for a serious relationship and I know I have some skeletons to bury. I don't know where my career is going or whether the army will keep me."

Jan looked at him, shaking her head. "Yes, we do need to talk. I am tired of being alone. I want to live life again. What I'm confused about is how you feel about me."

They looked into each other's eyes, and each saw the feeling of desperation they shared. Hal wanted to stand and take her in his arms. He knew what his body wanted, he had never met a woman that could excite him the way Jan did. He wanted her but only if she wanted him and could accept him the way he was. Was she feeling she owed him something? Did she feel sorry for him? How could he be sure? Better yet, could she be sure?

But then if he had not seen her nude on the beach about to be raped and beat off her attackers they would never have met. Had she just been a beautiful neighbor on the beach he knew he would have kept to himself. He was just not ready to be with other people. There were too many ghosts and too much pain. In Afghanistan he had lost too many friends. His life was off the rails and it would take time to return to some semblance of normalcy.

His ex-wife came to mind. Did he want to go through that again? Would Jan turn out to be the domineering money-hungry obese bitch that Muriel had become? He remembered coming home from a tour of duty in Cyprus to discover his wife had cleaned out his bank account and spent it all on clothes and another diamond ring. She had cleaned out the garage and thrown away things he had treasured since childhood. Their credit cards were maxed out and she had the guts to tell him to get another job to pay for her lifestyle. It had taken him years to pay off the debt and he was still stuck with the alimony payments. The fact that there were no kids involved was either an act of God or pure blind bullshit luck.

Realizing he had been staring out to sea he turned to speak to Jan but she was gone. Through the window he could see her at the table in her kitchen. She appeared to be staring into the jungle. Hal rose and folded his chair. He had no choice but to go to town. He was out of water. The toilet was so full it was ready to overflow. Without propane he had no refrigerator, or stove to cook on. Besides he was out of beer and had next to nothing left to eat. After stowing the lawn chair in the camper he looked up at the coconuts in the tree above him. He could just leave and keep going. To another beach or another state it didn't matter one way or the other. But then his conscience jumped in and sideswiped him.

Would she be okay? Hal doubted if the shrimpers would be back. The odds were against another similar event. But should he leave her here alone? Or did he even want to? He knew he was just delaying things as he checked the truck tires, the motor oil and the radiator. Deep in thought he leaned against the front of the truck and glanced toward the water.

To his surprise a boat had arrived just beyond the reef. He heard the clatter of chain as the anchor splashed into the sea. It was more of a ship than a mere boat; Hal estimated it to be at least 65 feet long. A Hatteras? he thought, or perhaps a Choy Lee? Recalling his favorite boat manufacturers. The decks appeared to be either teak or mahogany. From the deck to the water line she glistened in stark white. Her reflection appeared in the calm waters. On deck and at the bow and stern were gleaming brass fittings. She appeared to be an older vessel but in immaculate condition. Obviously kept by an owner that cared. He turned his attention back to the motor home. With a defining slap on his truck's engine hood he strode toward the RV.

"Jan," he called from outside the screen door. "I do have to go to town. Do you need to go in, or can I get anything for you?" There was no reply. "Well I am going. If you're still here when I get back we can have that talk."

There was still no reply.

* * * *

A little later, while driving through jungle, he realized he missed her already. What if she was gone when he got back? Well, at least that would answer the question of how she felt. And if she were there, what would he say? If ever he had been in a catch 22 situation, this was it. By the time he reached Lazarro Cardenas he had made up his mind.

Instead of driving all the way to Chetumal he would stop at the run down RV Park at the junction. There he could dump his tanks and fill with water. At the small Mercado there he could purchase some bread, canned goods, and maybe some meat. There were very few places in Mexico where a shopper couldn't get propane and beer. Hell he might even grab a jug of Aguardiente. He had grown fond of the forty percent alcohol brewed from local sugarcane. It was a poor man's tequila but it made a great margarita. On impulse he bought some limes, bananas, a can of chili con carne and a stack of tortillas. Whether Jan was gone or not he could eat, drink and relax.

The young lady at the cash register was more than good looking and friendly. She had helped him find what he needed. He paid for his purchases and gave her a ten Peso tip. That brought a big smile and a cheerful, "Gracias!"

Retracing his route he soon left the highway and once again followed the jungle trail. Throwing caution to the wind he opened a can of ice cold Pacifico. Taking several long hard pulls on the beer it was soon gone, but he felt better for it. By late afternoon he arrived back on the beach. The RV was still there. He pulled into his earlier spot under the palms and killed the engine. With the case of beer under one arm and his groceries in the other he walked to the back door of the camper. With his purchases put away he busied himself installing the newly filled propane tanks and lighting the burner in the fridge. Opening a second beer he glanced out the window toward Jan's house on wheels.

She sat on the couch, reading. With the lawn chair in his hand he climbed down from the camper. The thoughts and feelings from earlier in the day flooded back. Nothing had been solved and nothing had really changed. Should he go to her or ignore her?

Chapter Twelve

Hal nursed another beer while watching the boat in the bay. There was some activity on the rear deck but he wasn't paying much attention. His mind ticked over the pros and cons of a relationship with Jan. Of course none of it mattered if she had no serious interest in him. He was trying to decide whether or not to go and talk to her when he heard her voice behind him.

"That's a nice looking boat. I wonder where it's from." She said, unfolding her lawn chair. She set it in the sand close to Hal and sat down. "Dick and I had a boat once but nothing like that."

Hal crunched the empty can with his good hand. He held up the other one for her to see. "I used to be able to do that with either hand. But then there are a lot of things I used to be able to do."

She shook her head and picked up a piece of shell from the beach. Turning it over and brushing off the sand she sighed and paused. "You know Hal, we both have problems. Most of yours are visible but mine aren't."

Hal raised his hand and looked her in the eye. He was about to speak and she stopped him.

"Let me finish!" An unusually sharp edge came into her voice. "You're sinking into a well of self-pity and shame. Yes, you are hurt! Yes, you are missing a foot and a couple of fingers; your scars are still fresh and ugly. But Hal you are alive! I would give anything to have had my husband come home with both arms and legs blown off. But he didn't and I buried him! The other day you said how lucky you were compared to the guys that didn't make it. You said you came to this beach to swim and get back in shape. I think you came here to hide!"

She was angry now, and intended to fire both barrels at him. "I don't think you want to be with people. In fact you're probably wishing you were somewhere else when I was attacked. Not an hour goes by that I don't think of you beating those guys off. I thank God you were near. If you hadn't been I would probably be dead by now."

Her voice began to shake. Several days of fear, anger and concern were finally coming out.

"Hal, they're wounds of honor, you should be proud of what you did over there. You are a soldier, you served the people of Canada and you paid a price. Whether you like it or not you are a hero, and a Veteran, and you were long before that night on the beach. So now you want to know where we stand? Well, so do I! Your wounds don't matter to me. Yes I feel bad that you got hurt. But I don't feel pity. You make me feel proud, and not just of you, but of all the guys over there. Yes, even Dick. It's like he died protecting me. If you were all in one piece and we had met the same way we would still be asking the same questions. It is called communicating, getting to know each other. We're no different than a million other couples, wondering where it will lead."

He listened and watched as the tears began. The sparkling drops leaving wet trails on her skin as they ran to her chin. Jan sniffed and dabbed her nose with a soggy tissue.

"If it really matters to you, I do care for you. Not in pity, and not just for helping me either. Do I love you? I don't know, at least not yet. You said you didn't even know my name. Well it is now, um, Janice Allison Northwaite. I'm sorry, but I didn't have time to introduce my self properly when we met. Do I want to be with you? For now, yes, I do. But first I have to know how you feel. Can you understand that?"

Hal sat for a moment, wanting to be sure she was finished before he replied. He was fingering the scar where he once had two fingers. Something in her voice didn't sound right. The way she said her name, she seemed to hesitate.

"Jan I think you're the best thing that could have happened to me. On the other hand, yes, I am feeling sorry for myself. But it's not because I got hurt in combat, and it's not because I am crippled or disabled. Maybe I am. But it doesn't really bother me. What really does bother me is being with you. Other people may point and gawk at me, I can handle that. But you deserve a guy that's all in one piece. You don't need people feeling sorry for you because of me. Do I care for you? Yes! Dammit! You are a wonderful woman. You're smart, good looking, and sexy as hell. But am I in love with you? I don't know either. I guess time will tell for both of us. For now I just want to be near you. But you are right; I picked this area so I could be alone. Not only that but I love to swim in the nude. It's something I can't do on a crowded beach, and haven't done since you came along."

He sat back in his chair, glad they had both cleared the air a bit. She came over and kneeled in front of him. Taking both his hands in hers she looked up, the tears still flowing.

"Hal, you're a wonderful man! Not just because you rescued me, but other things. You taught me to snorkel and shared your world with me. You're a great cook. Each day I learn more about you and you seem to be able to do almost anything. Can we just go with the flow and see where it leads us? Please?"

Despite his best efforts Hal could no longer hold back his emotions. The tears ran down his face as he leaned forward and kissed her.

"Okay!"

He said simply, and that said it all. Both remained silent for a few moments. Suddenly Hal pointed at the water and said, "Hey watch this!"

Jan turned, looking to where he was pointing. On the back of the yacht two people were standing at an opening in the starboard railing. They were dressed in diving gear and preparing to enter the water. First one, then the other stepped forward, turned around, and jumped backward into the water. The air tanks on their backs were the first to hit the surface, in a moment they had disappeared. "SCUBA!" said Hal. "I think you would love it.

"Maybe." replied Jan, "I am willing to try almost anything once.

"I think we need to go into the city," Hal mused, a plan forming in his head.

"To Chetumal?" quizzed Jan.

"No, not Chetumal," said Hal in a teasing voice.

"Playa del Carman?" she tried.

"No, again," came his reply. "I think it is time we headed for the bright lights. How about a few days in Cancun?"

Jan looked at him and smiled. "That sounds like fun. Did you have anything in mind?"

Returning the smile, Hal replied, "As a matter of fact I do." He gasped both her hands in both of his. It was the first time he had touched her with the three-fingered hand. "How long has it been since you were on a date? Like a real date? I want to take you out to dinner and then maybe try some dancing. At least I think I can dance with this peg leg."

Squeezing his hand in response, Jan's face lit up. The smile broadened and her eyes grew wide. Her heart was pounding, she loved to dance and never dreamed Hal would want to go. "When do we leave?" she asked.

"How about right after lunch? It is about a three-hour drive and we want to get there before dark. We can scout the place tomorrow and go out tomorrow night. While we're there we need to see if we can come up with some diving gear."

Jan jumped to her feet. "Then I had better start getting ready. How about a corned beef on rye for lunch?" Hal just grinned; this girl already knew his favorites. By the time the next few days were over they would know a lot more about each other's likes, and dislikes.

As she entered the coach she called back over her shoulder, "And just so you know, I happen to like skinny-dipping also."

Her last comment hit Hal like a hammer. His libido kicked up a notch at the thought of them diving naked together. The thing with her name came to mind again. Did he hear her wrong the first time? Then she had said her ex-husband. Was he dead or wasn't he? Something about this woman just didn't seem right.

Chapter Thirteen

The mid-afternoon traffic in Cancun caught Jan by surprise. She had expected a typical Mexican city, narrow streets, older buildings, and poverty. As she followed Hal's truck they drove down a modern four lane super highway. The center median was planted with tall, mature palms.

They were heading toward an RV park Hal knew of on the north side of town. As they passed the area known by tourists as "The Strip" she gaped at the tall elegant looking buildings. There seemed to be miles of fancy new hotels along the beach. It was more like a coastal town in south Florida than in Mexico.

Leaving the downtown area, Hal soon pulled into an old, well-used park. He stopped near the office and walked back to the coach. "It don't look like much but it's clean, and cheap, has good water and the power is pretty safe." He offered.

Jan had discovered while driving across Mexico that local water was often polluted. The electrical connections were notorious for poor grounding and voltage surges. Most tourists, including her, bought purified water in twenty-three liter jugs for drinking and cooking. While waiting for Hal to come back from the office she took in the surroundings. Through the palms at the back of the park she could see the sea. In the distance she could see an island and wondered if it was inhabited.

Hal knocked on the side window interrupting her daydreaming. She slid the glass back in order to hear him.

"You're going into spot number six, and I am right next door in number four. It will cost you a hundred pesos a day." He instructed, pointing toward the assigned locations.

"So how long are we staying? How much should I pay for?"

Hal just smiled, "What am I the tour guide? I told him we would pay before we leave."

Jan started the engine and backed into her assigned slot. Next they busied themselves with the menial tasks of connecting the water, sewer, and electrical services.

By the time she was finished Hal was set up and engaged in a conversation with a gray-haired man parked on the other side. She walked over and said hello, just to be neighborly. They were discussing eating-places, prices, and quality. Apparently the older gentleman had been here for several months and had sampled much of the local cuisine. As they walked back to their spots she mentioned the island she could see.

"That's Isla Mujeres," replied Hal. "It means Island of Women and some say it was once reserved for prostitutes."

"But does anyone live there?" She queried.

"Oh yes, there is a town and lots of homes and cottages. It's kind of a fun place. There are ferries running back and forth every hour or so. We can go over there before we leave Cancun if you like. Anyway, if you want to change before we go, we could wander downtown and see what we can find for excitement."

It didn't take Jan long to change and get ready. She emerged wearing pale green slacks and a white blouse.

Hal had also changed and was waiting for her at

the picnic table. He was wearing light tan trousers and a white pullover polo shirt. Following his example she locked her coach and joined him. Together they walked out of the park and down the street toward the strip.

From the bars and restaurants came the sounds of Mexican music. People were singing, laughing and joking; everyone sounded in a party mood. Hal grasped her hand with his good right one.

"So do you want to eat Mexican, European, or American? He asked. Jan hesitated for a moment before laughing and giving him a reply.

"Oh hell, we might as well eat the local stuff. It can only kill us." A few minutes later he led her into the dining room of an upscale hotel on the beach. The Maitre'd seated them near a window facing the sea and a waiter appeared from nowhere.

"Anything special you'd like to have or shall I just order for both of us." He asked.

"Go for it!" She ordered. "Surprise me, I'm up for anything."

Hal turned to the waiter and ordered a bottle of white wine. He then asked for ceviche, and Chilies Rellenos. Jan had no idea what was coming. They sipped the wine and watched as Para Gliders flew up and down the beach, parachutes towed by powerboats. A few minutes later their appetizers arrived.

"Ahh, ceviche." Hal smiled at her as the waiter placed the dishes before them. "Now you want to take that sliced lime and squeeze the juice over the vegetables. It not only perks up the flavor, it's a natural disinfectant. It will take care of any germs on the salad. The seafood is marinated in lime juice before it is added."

Jan poked her fork through the mixture, she found chilies, tomato, cilantro, onion, and chopped seafood presented in a large goblet. Taking a small taste she nodded and smiled. "This is very good, and I've never had it before. It tastes like a bit of olive oil and lime is mixed in it."

Hal returned her smile, "It's called ceviche. It's very popular along the coasts where seafood is plentiful. But wait until you taste the Rellenos. They're my favorite!"

What had appeared to Jan to be a very large salad soon disappeared as she enjoyed the unique taste. She had no sooner finished than the waiter appeared with two large plates. They were on a serving cart accompanied by a series of smaller plates and bowls.

"This is a local variation of chilies Rellenos," explained Hal. "I have had them all over Mexico. No two places make them the same except they all use the same poblano pepper."

Jan glanced at the rest of the dishes. There were nachos and salsa, sliced limes, guacamole, a plate of sliced raw vegetables, and a bowl of sour cream. She lifted the cover on a foam plastic container and found it held a stack of warm tortillas. On her plate was what she assumed was the Rellenoe. It looked like a deflated balloon deep-fried in batter. Around the pepper were several tamales, still wrapped in the traditional cornhusks. To the side was a large scoop of refried beans.

"Wow," she muttered, "There is enough here for a family of five."

She watched Hal as he used a nacho to scoop up a load of salsa and she followed suit. They repeated the process and tasted the guacamole. Next Hal lifted a corner of a cornhusk and let the tamale unroll. He spooned on a dollop of sour cream followed by a splash of salsa verde.

"The red salsa is a little milder," he advised, "But the green one is called salsa verde, and it is pretty hot.

In Spanish it is described as piquante."

Jan took a little of the green mixture on a taco and tried it. She was soon reaching for the glass of water in front of her. Hal tried the battered chili. Then he tore off a piece of tortilla and scooped up a spoonful of refried beans. Jan followed his example. They ate in silence except for the odd "Mmmm," from Jan, as she tasted something new. She ate until she could eat no more and sipped on her wine.

"That is so good," she exclaimed, "But I can't eat another bite. I feel like a just had a full course Christmas dinner. Do you suppose they have doggie bags?"

Hal laughed, his mouth full of tamale and salsa. "I don't think so," he said, after swallowing. "Besides why have leftovers when we can have something different tomorrow?" As the sun set over Yucatan Channel, they finished their meal and the last of the wine. While Hal paid the check a mariachi band started playing on the patio near the beach.

"Want to go for a walk?" he asked, returning to her side.

She took his hand, the left one this time. And headed out the door. When they reached the beach she removed her shoes and carried them by the straps.

"These high heels just don't work in sand."

As the sky grew darker more lights appeared. Hal pointed to Isla Mujeres where the beach was now a sparkling mass of lights.

"Mujeres!" he explained. "And over there is Cozumel, a much larger island and more like Cancun."

The lights from hotels, restaurants and bars followed the line of the beach until they disappeared from sight. The air seemed alive with the sounds of Mexican music and singers. There were people everywhere, walking, talking, or just sitting on the sand. She could pick out voices in English, French, German, and of course Spanish. "There must be hundreds," she whispered, "If not thousands of people staying in all these hotels."

A fireworks display began on the beach nearby. Hal guided her to a bench where they could sit and watch. As she sidled up close to him he put his arm around her.

In response she tilted her head and leaned it on his shoulder. The bottle rockets soared aloft with a screaming wail and trailing sparks before bursting in a dazzling display of colored stars. Occasionally the deeper boom of a mortar shell echoed down the beach. Following the sound a massive eruption of multi-colored explosions appeared against the black sky.

The flashing and banging lasted about fifteen minutes. Then the stench of gunpowder hung over the beach in a thick white cloud. They left the bench and resumed their walk. Toward the end of the strip they found themselves in front of a small bar.

"A nightcap?" suggested Hal.

Sure!" she willingly replied and they stepped inside. After placing their orders Hal noticed a small dance floor. A Jukebox was playing a soft slow sixties tune. Smiling, he reached his hand across the table.

"I think I'd like to try dancing if you'll join me." Jan was amazed at his suggestion, with his foot she had never thought of him being a dancer. They rose and walked to the floor, there was no one else dancing. "I might stumble a bit," he joked. "I have never done this on one foot before."

They joined arms and began. Unsure of just where his foot was Hal bumped her ankle several times. He kept saying he was sorry and was just about to give up.

Sensing his discomfort, Jan moved in closer. She

guided his left leg with her right knee, helping him control where his foot went. They were soon waltzing as if they had been together for years.

Hal pulled her closer. Her knee rubbing on his was creating a reaction that was about to become obvious to her. He could feel the heat of her breasts on his chest, and smell the fresh clean aroma of her newly shampooed hair. It had been several years since he had last danced. Until tonight he had never thought he would dance again. The song ended and they wandered back, arm-in-arm, to their table.

"That was nice." He said simply. "Thank you."

"Well my ankle might be black and blue tomorrow, but I enjoyed it too." She had that pixie-like grin that he'd come to love on her face. They danced several more times until Jan realized Hal was beginning to limp.

"Honey, your leg!" she blurted before realizing what she had said.

"It's okay," he stated, also surprised at the way she had addressed him. "I guess dancing uses different muscles than walking. The stump is starting to bother me."

Jan waved to the waiter. As he approached she spoke, "Taxi, por favor." Hal could not believe what she had done.

"We don't need a taxi, I am quite capable of walking back.

"Hal it is more than a mile back to the park. Now quit trying to be a hero. I know you could walk it but then tomorrow you will be so sore you won't want to do anything. Besides, my feet are getting sore also. I haven't worn high heels this much for years."

He squared up the bar tab with the waiter just as the" taxi" arrived. It was an old style Volkswagen beetle. The front passenger seat had been removed to allow easy access to the back seat. The two Canadians looked at the car and then each other in disbelief. Then Jan jumped in and Hal followed her. The driver spoke reasonable English so there was no problem telling him where they wanted to go.

"You know, he said as he squirmed into the little car. "In Mexico City they call these cabs 'Hitler's Revenge'"

They had not gone far when Hal felt Jan's hand on his knee. "Thank you for tonight," she offered. "It's been a very long time since I did anything like that."

Hal placed his hand over hers, squeezing gently. "Who knows," he responded, "Maybe we'll get to like it enough to do it again." He leaned over and kissed her on the forehead just as the driver reported, "Senor, nosotros aqui!"

Hal paid the man and they walked through the park gate to the RVs.

"Now it's my turn," announced Jan. "Will you join me for a nightcap?"

Chapter Fourteen

Hal relaxed on the couch and watched as Jan mixed the drinks. He admired her shape and felt his body reacting to her. Moving on impulse he approached her. Putting his hands on her hips he nuzzled the back of her neck.

Jan stopped what she was doing for a moment, briefly enjoying his embrace. Hal turned her around and cupped her face in his hands. She lifted her lips as he lowered his mouth towards hers. As their lips touched they each felt an electric spark. His tongue gently teased her lips. She responded by openly her lips and allowing him deeper access. His arms slipped around her waist, pulling her to him. Her hands wrapped around his neck hungrily enjoying the moment.

The embrace continued until Jan gently pushed on his shoulders, breaking the kiss. "Slow down soldier, the ice is melting in your glass, and our drinks are getting warm."

"That's not all that's getting warm." He whispered under his breath. Hal kissed her on the forehead before stepping away. He returned to the couch and Jan sat in the easy chair. "I couldn't resist that, you just look so delicious. It was a real treat to dance with you tonight."

Jan smiled and blushed slightly, "Well I enjoyed our date also, and we'll have to try dancing again." She lifted her glass and sipped its contents. Hal did likewise never shifting his eyes from hers.

"So what would you like to do tomorrow?" He asked, in an attempt to break the uncomfortable silence.

Jan thought for a moment, wondering what there was to do in Cancun. "Maybe some shopping," she offered. "If we're going to continue doing the beach thing I need to pick up a better pair of shoes, and a beach jacket. Then maybe grab a few groceries, some Pacifico beer for my honey, and maybe a couple of steaks."

As soon as she said it she realized she had again used a more intimate term. Despite her reservations she seemed to be falling for this guy and she still wondered if it were a good thing. Her extended leave would soon run out and she hadn't decided whether to continue her career or leave the army.

Hal had heard what she said and liked it. He was thinking of a way to return the greeting in a similar fashion. "Okay sweetheart, I need to do some shopping also." Hal wondered where there was a dive shop and if he might be able to rent some scuba gear. It would be too expensive to buy new equipment that would have to come later. But they could have some fun shopping at the bazaar in the Mexican quarter away from the main street along the strip. There were so many items that just could not be found anywhere else. And the prices were much lower than the stores where most of the tourists shopped.

He also wanted to check on the schedule for the ferry to Isla Mujeres. He finished his drink and put the empty glass on the counter. "Well my dear it's getting late. I need to get some sleep and take this foot off for a while." He leaned over and kissed her on the forehead.

She smiled, "Thank you again for a wonderful evening and I'll see you tomorrow." She was still not quite ready to have him in her bed.

* * * *

The coming of dawn found Hal still in bed. The activities of the previous day had relaxed him more than he had been in many months. His feelings toward Jan were becoming more intense. He felt hers were also. He felt comfortable with everything they did. She had enjoyed what he had enjoyed. He admired the fact that she was ready to try anything. She certainly appeared to be his kind of woman.

After breakfast at her place Hal suggested they take his truck downtown. It was a long way to walk back carrying a load of groceries and whatever else they found. Hal puttered around a booth whose owner sold belt buckles while Jan tried to find a pair of beach shoes at the next kiosk. He had almost decided on one when a familiar voice from behind startled him.

"Well I'll be damned." Said a female, "What the hell are you doing here?"

Hal whirled to face the voice from his past, hoping he was wrong. What he saw confirmed his fears. He was face-to-face with his ex-wife. She was the size of a small truck and wearing a light green print dress that could have doubled as a circus big top. She reached out to hug him but he drew back. She had been overweight when he saw her last but now she was just plain obese. Hal grimaced as he realized she must now weigh over three hundred pounds.

"Hello Muriel," was the only response he could muster. He couldn't imagine what the weight was doing to her health. He feared for her well being while they were married, in spite of her heartless treatment of his bank account. The poor woman needed help now more than ever.

"Where are the fingers?" She asked, in the belligerent tone that Hal remembered too well.

"I left them in Afghanistan, along with my left foot and some other pieces, not that you would give a damn anyway. Besides, we're divorced and it's none of your damned business." It was as if they were still married, always a conflict, no matter the subject.

Jan was approaching from behind Muriel and had heard the last bit of the conversation. She stepped around the obese monster and put her arm around Hal's waist.

"C'mon darling'." Her voiced dripped honey. "The kids will be waiting for us, we had better go."

Not believing his ears Hal threw the briefest smile in Muriel's direction and walked away. The last he remembered of Muriel was her multi-leveled chin dropping almost to her chest in pure disbelief. He was having a difficult time suppressing the laughter in his throat.

"Well, honey" he emphasized the endearment. "That should raise some comments from her friends when she gets home. You should get an Oscar for that performance.

"Wow!" Chortled Jan. "Has she always been that big? And that obnoxious?"

"Believe it or not she was barely a hundred pounds when we got married. Two years later she was up to one fifty. She just did nothing but eat and bitch about my job. We started to fight about her eating us out of house and home and me being away too much. Then the credit card and bank account thing happened and I left her. I have no idea how or why she came to be in Cancun."

They walked toward the hotel where Hal had parked the truck. Along the way they stopped at a Mercado and bought the groceries they needed. Jan was deep in thought as they loaded the truck and climbed aboard.

"Have you ever thought of getting married again?"

she asked suddenly.

"Not really!" he answered, "At least not until lately."

"Oh? To anyone I know?" She was teasing him.

"I think you know her very well." Hal responded as he pulled out into the afternoon traffic. "The problem is I don't think she knows it yet, and I'm not sure if she is ready for a serious commitment. The rest of the return trip passed in silence, each of them considering the ramifications of the last topic.

Arriving at the RV Park they found a piece of paper stuck under the wiper of Jan's coach. It referred to a question he had asked at a dive shop earlier. A printed advertisement, it described their services. They had a fully certified instructor, several dive boats, rental equipment, and a properly maintained air compressor for filling the dive tanks.

"So, are you still up for some real diving?" He asked.

"In the water?" She joked.

"Well yes, unless you would like to dive somewhere else." The banter continued. "You will have to take a short course before they can rent you the gear but I can teach you everything you need to know beforehand. They have to do it by law; I want to do it because I want you to be safe. It is a little more complicated and dangerous than snorkeling." He paused to hear her response. "But if you like we could go to bed instead?"

Jan smiled, "I will take that under consideration. An offer like that doesn't come along every day. At least I don't think I will be facing any competition from your ex."

Hal choked on the mouthful of beer he had just taken. Swallowing with some difficulty he laughed and simply replied. "Uh, No."

With the groceries put away Jan began to prepare

their evening meal. Hal sat back and watched. "You know," he began, "If your cooking is as good as your looks, I just may have to move in."

Jan turned and stared at him. Her hand held the spatula up in the air as she prepared herresponse. Then she smiled, shook her head and replied.

"No comment!" Hal watched her as his mind probed the possibility. Marriage was still a forbidden subject. But could he and Jan continue to be this happy if they just lived together? There was one main question that really bothered him. Was Jan ready to share her bed?

Chapter Fifteen

The next morning, a beautiful red sunrise welcomed Hal as he stepped down from his camper.

He had already enjoyed toast and coffee so he busied himself preparing for their planned outing. A quick look toward Jan's coach revealed a kitchen light; she too, had risen early. Hal removed a red backpack from the cab of his truck and started packing it for the days' trek with a blanket, insect repellent, a compass, his knife and several cans of beer. Finally, he strapped his machete to the pack. Dressed in jeans and a long-sleeved denim shirt he felt prepared for their planned day in the jungle.

Jan, stepping down from the coach, carried several articles to the picnic table. "Good morning, Bwana Hal."

Hal chuckled, "Me not Bwana, me Tarzan, you Jane."

"Well Tarzan, I made sandwiches for lunch. For dessert I have a couple of oranges, two bananas, and a bottle of that German wine. Do you have more of those good crystal plastic wine glasses?" She joked.

After retrieving the glasses from the camper he began to pack her supplies. "You look as good as ice cream on a hot day." She looked trim and slim in yellow slacks, and matching blouse. "I love the earrings too." He nodded, recognizing the cowry shells. Their preparations complete, they climbed into the cab of his old truck.

After Hal had started the engine she asked, "So how far is it to Tixmul? "

"About a hundred and fifty Kilometers we should be there in about two hours." As they left the jungle trail, the smoother road continued to wind through the canopied forest. While rounding a curve Hal suddenly swerved to avoid a large mat of woven palm leaves on the highway.

Jan turned for a better look as they went by. "What is that stuff?"

Hal smiled, returning the truck to its proper lane. "The locals pick wild coffee beans and the road is the only space with enough sun to dry them. There are natives living in shacks through here to be close to the wild coffee.

"I wonder if the kids, dogs, and other animals scampering across the mat would affect the flavor of the coffee?" She mused. As if emphasizing her observation several loose ranging cattle along the road were walking on the beans.

"Oh my God! Look!" Jan gasped, pointing at a native woman hanging laundry on a line. "She's half naked. Oh, Um, Tarzan you just keep your eyes on the road."

Hal smiled, "Yes, I saw her too." Just before ten o'clock they turned off at the sign for Tixmul. Finding a shady spot, Hal stopped in the crude parking area. "We're the only ones here," he said, turning off the engine. "This is it, end of the line, everyone out."

* * * *

Jan just stood by the truck for a moment, taking in the view. "These ancient ruins have always amazed me. The Mayans were like the Egyptians. Their pyramids were also constructed without heavy equipment. They defy explanation. Can you imagine building this place with your bare hands?"

Slipping the backpack over his shoulder Hal

locked the truck before replying. "No, I can't, and look at the detail in the carvings." He was pointing to the scene above them. The walls and buildings, carved from solid rock, hung with vines as the jungle struggled to reclaim the ruins of this once proud city. Iguanas scattered at their approach and monkeys howled from the treetops. Flashes of color through the trees announced the arrival of parrots, macaws, and finches.

"They expect a handout of peanuts or bananas from tourists." he said. Taking Jan's hand in his, and he led her forward. "The best is yet to come." He offered.

Her head pivoting from side to side she followed his finger as he pointed out interesting objects. They passed an observatory, several altars, and an ancient form of basketball court. In just the few years since finding this lost city, archeologists had removed the heaviest of jungle overgrowth.

"Everything is just as they left it, just like Palenque and Teotihuacan." Jan stated. "So you've been there?" he asked. "

Yes, on the way down here. I heard one guy say it was no big deal, just a pile of rocks."

"Well you know, some people have no respect for anything." They had explored the city for a couple of hours when Hal asked if she was hungry.

"Famished!" Jan admitted.

"Then come with me." He ordered, removing a folded paper from his pocket.

"What is that? It looks like a map."

"A friend was here several years ago and told me about this place." Began Hal. "He drew this map for me and said to be sure to visit this spot. I don't know what's there, but it shouldn't be far."

Following the rough, hand drawn map, it led them to an opening in the city's outer wall. Hidden by a large monolith, it took Hal a few minutes to locate it. He ducked behind the stone and disappeared. A moment later his arm appeared through the green foliage as he reached for her hand.

Jan had to bend down to scurry through a small tunnel under the wall. Beyond the wall they emerged in a tiny clearing outside the ruins. Consulting the map, Hal unsheathed the razor sharp machete. "This way." He said, folding the map. He had to swing the blade often to clear a path through the new growth concealing their route.

Jan found the trail too narrow to walk hand in hand. She followed close behind. Twenty minutes later they reached a surprising destination.

Captivated and speechless they stared at the scene before them. They were at the edge of a fairly large clearing. Several minutes passed before Jan whispered, "Wow!

"Roger that!" Was all Hal could manage, reverting to the military vernacular. At the far side, beyond a carpet of soft green grass, lay a glistening sapphire pool among moss-covered rocks. From above a tiny waterfall fell like a bridal veil, before striking the surface. Hal removed his pack and placed it on one of the rocks before extracting the folded blanket.

Together they spread the deep red material on the grass. Hal opened the wine and poured a glass for each of them. Meanwhile Jan unwrapped the sandwiches.

"It's like the Garden of Eden must have been." She whispered softly. They ate silently, each engrossed in the pristine beauty and serenity of this hidden wonderland. Occasionally a gentle breeze swept across the clearing causing the delicate fall of water to sway to and fro. Hal leaned back against the rock and slipped his arm around her. She leaned into his shoulder; it had been a long time since she had felt this relaxed. With his injured hand he lifted her chin and turned her head. She looked into his eyes as they kissed. It started out as a brief friendly exchange until his tongue brushed her lips.

She felt the tingling begin as she returned his gentle probing. Hal broke off the kiss. He put both his arms around her and lay back on the blanket pulling her with him. He rolled sideways and they were now face to face. He nuzzled her ear. His hot breath on her neck created more trembles. From her ear he slowly moved to her throat, kissing gently, one side then the other. He too was feeling the effect and knew it would be obvious to her before long. He raised his body and placed Jan on her back. Lowering his head again he sought her lips. She felt his hand move up her side, his thumb stroking a now sensitive nipple.

Jan moaned softly, her body reacting to feelings she had denied herself for so long. She held him close with one arm while with the other she ran her hand through his hair. Growing bolder he gently cupped her breast. He felt the growing hardness of the erect nipple. Starting at the top he began undoing buttons on her blouse. As the soft yellow cotton fell away he lifted her slightly and reached behind to unhook her bra.

"It's on the front," she whispered.

Surprised, he located the fastener and released it. The sudden release of her breasts was a pleasure beyond his dreams. They were perfect twins with long hard nipples protruding from matching pink aureoles. He slid down again, kissing his way from her neck to her naked breasts.

Jan moaned as he took first one and then the other nipple in his lips. He kissed and sucked gently, stroking each in turn with his tongue.

She held his head, pulling him tightly against her aching breasts. Hal slowly slid his hand down across her belly. Gently rubbing the yellow slacks covering her most tender parts. Again and again he ran his hand over the swollen mound marking her womanhood.

"I want to kiss you," he whispered, "There."

He pressed his fingers against her. She pulled his head up from her breast and kissed his lips, this time her tongue began the probing exploration. Hal unsnapped her slacks and slid down the zipper. She kicked off her shoes as he gently slid the material down and off. Moving with the frenzy born of the moment she grasped his shirt. With one decisive pull she separated all the snaps. He shrugged out of the unwanted garment.

Moving down between her legs he slowly began peeling down her panties. She lifted slightly to help him. At her feet he dropped the wispy underwear and kissed her ankles, one then the other. He moved up her legs kissing each in turn. At her knees he pressed gently and she opened herself to him. As he kissed his way up her inner thighs his good hand was working at his waist. He soon had his zipper down and managed to wriggle out of trousers and briefs.

Feeling his breath on her Jan reached down and pulled his head to her waiting mound. Kissing first, then licking, he found her engorged clitoris and took it in his lips. As she thrust against him he slipped a finger into her, then another. While exploring her hot wet channel he brushed against her G-spot. Her response was an instantaneous orgasmic clenching of vaginal muscle. He was taking her to a level she had never achieved before.

While busily tonguing and fingering her wet and dripping sex he slowly rotated himself around. He positioned himself upside down to her.

Jan turned her head and found his massive erection nearly poking her in the eye. Though she had never tasted a man before she kissed the thick purple head presented to her. His taste and feel drove her beyond reason. She took him in her mouth but found there was too much of him. She sucked and licked just as he was doing to her.

Hal lifted up and turned to face her. Resting on outstretched arms he looked into her eyes as he lowered himself. With legs spread wide and knees bent she arched her back to meet him.

"Yes," she whispered, "Please, yes, now."

She watched while he produced a condom and put it on. He slipped into her and gently pushed, but shallow at first. She felt so tight he was afraid he might hurt her. Giving her half of his length he stopped, allowing her a moment to adjust to his size. Slowly, a little at a time, he went deeper. She had never felt so filled.

As he eased the last of his erection into her he felt a restriction. He had come to her cervix; she was completely and totally filled.

Hal began a rhythmic motion, pulling almost all the way out before plunging in again. She began to move with him, her hips lifting to meet his. She had lost what little control she had left. An orgasm more massive than any she had ever known raged through her. Her hips were bucking, her vagina pulsing with contractions. She was breathing fast, panting, unable to catch her breath.

"Bingo!" She shouted, "Ohhh, bingo, bingo, bingo!"

Her vaginal contractions were enough to overcome Hal's willpower. He tried to hold back but her body was milking him. It was the softest, most velvety place he could imagine. She felt the hot spurts as jet after jet of his seed sprayed toward her womb. He lowered himself to her, his chest crushing her breasts, as he worked her clitoris with his pelvis. Her subsiding orgasm renewed itself as again and again he brought her to a cataclysmic and satisfying series of contractions. She felt her vagina grasp him in a series of muscular waves as her world exploded around her like fireworks on the Fourth of July. They remained lying side by side, both still breathing hard.

Hal rolled to face her, kissed her tenderly, and whispered the words she had waited so long to hear.

"I love you, Jan!

"And I love you too."

"That was the first time I ever did that, you know, with my mouth." She said.

His hand reached over and stroked her bare bottom. "Mmmmm, but you are so good." He replied.

"Maybe it was beginner's luck. Should we do it again?" She whispered. A hopeful note accented her question.

Chapter Sixteen

Hal rolled on his side and kissed her. With his breathing back to normal he was able to speak. "Beginner's luck huh? Well we will have to see."

She smiled and turned to face him, their bodies molding together. "I think that soldier of yours is ready for action." She pushed him onto his back and straddled him.

He fumbled in the backpack and found another condom. She took it from him and smiled. She tore open the foil packet and slipped it over him, slowly rolling it down his length. She sat up and rose to her knees.

"My turn," She said as she lowered herself onto him. "

Hal reached up and cupped her breasts, "Mmmmm," was his only response. If she continued this he would again lose control.

She impaled herself on his spear, engulfing him completely. With slow teasing moves she began to lift and lower. She leaned forward until her breasts were stroking his chest, nipple to nipple.

Hal thrust upward as she slid down. The rhythm began, each matching the other. All other thoughts, sights and sounds disappeared. In the ecstatic throes of another orgasmic pinnacle their attention to each other outweighed everything.

They lay still at last, enjoying the after effects of their desires. As Hal's breathing slowed he looked into her eyes and smiled. "So are we going

to try for three out of three?"

She held his softened member in her hand, "Whenever he's up for it." She giggled.

They were laying the sun, enjoying a well-earned and needed rest. "Well now that we know each other better, we can skinny-dip together," he suggested.

Jan jumped up, laughing, "Last one in does the dishes." She was already running for the pool.

Hal rose to follow but she outran him. She ran out on a large rock and jumped. The splash had barely subsided when she surfaced with an ear- splitting scream.

Hal had just left the rock. He was going in, no matter what. As he entered the water he saw her heading for shore, her arms flailing. In an instant he knew the reason.

"Holy shit, it's freezing!" She screamed running for the blanket.

A split second later Hal surfaced. He too made for shore at record-breaking speed.

"Next time, check the water first," he cautioned. He was shivering when he reached Jan and shared the blanket "I guess it will have to be two out of three,"

She smiled as she looked down at his once proud penis. The cold water had deflated him and even his testicles had shrunk

"You never mentioned a time limit," his teeth chattered as he spoke. "And I think your girls got the same treatment." He bent to take a nipple in his lips. They were both rock hard and pointing straight out.

The sun had traversed the sky and the shadows grew longer. With the late afternoon came cooler air. Covered with goose bumps from their icy plunge they dressed quickly. A last look at the waterfall would be a memory they would never forget.

Once inside the wall, they strolled arm in arm

through the ancient city. Even a stranger would have noticed the sparkle in Jan's eyes and the spring in Hal's step. By the time they reached the truck and packed their gear the sun was beginning to set. As he started the engine she moved to the center and fastened the middle seat belt.

"It was a wonderful day, thank you." She laid her head against his shoulder.

"No sweetheart, thank you." He placed his hand on her thigh and squeezed gently. They were back on the highway when a thought occurred to him.

"Honey, what are we going to have for supper? Everything I have is frozen solid."

She thought for a moment, "I have a can or two of beans, and we could make toast."

"Well we passed a place at the junction. Judging by all the pickups and semi-trailers parked there the locals must like the food." He offered.

"Well if you know what to order. I'm lost when it comes to understanding food names. I can go along with tortilla, taco, frijoles, and cervesa. But when I look at a menu I am lost. Between empanada and empanizado and enparedado I might be ordering dog food for all I know."

"Well just please don't order Cabeza de Cabrito or I will be out of there in a flash."

"OK so what is this cabeza stuff?"

"Well, if you really want to know. They marinade and barbecue the head of a baby goat. Then they chop it in half so you can eat the contents.

"Yuk!" She replied. "That's gross."

"Yes, well if I even smell menudo I am gone. That stuff is made from cow stomach and all kinds of internal parts. It smells terrible. They say it is a sure cure for a hangover. If I had it for breakfast I would be hanging over all right."

They arrived at the dilapidated truck stop and

walked in. The woman at the stove greeted them in Spanish. "Do you speak English?" asked Hal. "Si, a little bit," she replied, and pointed to a vacant table. "Do you have quesadilla con pollo and tamales carne?" he queried.

"Si, in a small moment Senor."

"Y dos cervesa pacifico, por favor." He responded, ordering two beers.

The woman smiled, nodded, and merely answered "si" before returning to her stove. A

younger girl appeared a moment later and served them each a beer. There were no glasses and each bottle had a small wedge of lime inserted in the neck Jan looked at the bottle quizzically. She had never seen this done before.

"Remember when I said lime was a natural disinfectant? This way it means they have wiped the bottle with the lime and it is safe to drink from it." He extracted the lime and took a swig of the ice-cold contents.

Jan followed suit as the girl came back with the traditional Mexican appetizers; nachos, salsa, guacamole, and jalapenos.

"Gracias," responded Hal.

They munched on the snack and Jan noticed the floor. "It's a dirt floor" she retorted, a surprised look on her face.

"Yes it is." He agreed.

She looked around, taking in the rough, hand-hewn timbers and the roof thatched with palm leaves. The window openings had no glass and the doorway held no door. The tables and chairs were obviously hand made but the workmanship showed skill and care. From the ceiling hung two bare electric lights, but neither was turned on. Other than the compacted earth floor everything seemed clean. It was just so different from any restaurant she had ever seen.

Before long their food arrived, hot steaming, and smelling delicious. Jan had not realized how hungry she was until she started on the appetizers. Now she took a piece of the sliced quesadilla and ate it like she would a wedge of pizza. She recognized the cornhusk wrapped tamales from their last Mexican meal. This time she avoided the green Salsa Verde and chose the red variety instead. With her tamale unwrapped and layered with the sauce and sour cream she tried a forkful. Even the milder salsa brought tears to her eyes and she guzzled a long pull of her beer.

Hal chuckled, "The locals make salsa with more heat than the restaurants for tourists do. You could probably weld steel plate with the green one." He signaled the young waitress. "Mas cervesa por favor" he called. He too had emptied his beer trying to put out the fire. Jan gulped down a mouthful of tamale. Then, nearly choking, she pointed to a table near the door.

"Oh my God!" She exclaimed.

Under the table a kitten had dug a hole in the dirt. It now turned and made a deposit in the hole, burying the results with her front paws.

"Only in Mexico." Laughed Hal.

They finished their meal in silence and Hal paid the bill, leaving a ten-peso tip for the staff. The food was good, the service great, and the prices far below those in the city. The animal act with the kitten had been an unexpected bonus.

It was nearly dark when they arrived back at the beach. Hal parked the truck, put the trash from the day in his green bag, and stored the backpack. He called to her through the screen door,

"Everything okay in there?"

Her answer seemed muffled, "Come on in."

He climbed the steps and saw a dim light coming from her bedroom.

"In here honey." Jan was in bed, under the covers. The sheet was pulled down on the opposite side. Her bare arm appeared and she patted the lower sheet beside her "Do you still want to try and make it three out of three?" She asked, a devilish grin on her face.

Hal quickly stripped off his clothes and joined her. Under the sheet he found her warm, naked and ready. They snuggled into each other's arms and picked up where they had left off earlier. The effects of their icy dip in the jungle pool had now worn off. Her woman's juices were flowing and his man parts were answering her challenge. She repeated the ritual with the condom.

"I love you so much," she whispered as he slowly slid into her warm wet nook .

"And I love you, but this could get to be a habit."

She thrust upward to meet him. "Is that a promise?"

"Well it could be, but the condom department is going to be out of stock before long. I don't usually buy them by the dozen, or the gross."

Chapter Seventeen

As they passed through the last shopping area Hal pulled up in front of store bearing a large sign advertising Farmacia. Jan gave him a strange look.

"Drug store, I need to restock my condoms. Do you need anything?"

Jan blushed; their newfound intimacy had opened many doors. "You had better get a large box," she giggled.

Hal returned with a white paper bag clutched in one hand and a newspaper in the other. "They only had them in boxes of twelve," he grinned. "So I got three boxes. That should last until the weekend."

"By that time I'll be walking bowlegged," she laughed. "And you'll be wasted away to a shadow."

Hal displayed her favorite grin. "But what a way to go."

While she prepared their evening meal Hal was reading the Galveston Daily News. As was his old habit he began with the classifieds, specifically in the used boats section. Jan turned when she heard a low whistle. Hal had sat up and was circling an ad.

"I wonder if this boat has sold yet? Wow! What a deal. "

"What kind of boat?" she asked, thinking of a small outboard fishing boat.

"It is a forty foot C and C swing keel."He replied.

Jan frowned, "Which in English means exactly what? "

"It's a sail boat." He explained. "At forty feet she is the same size as your coach. The swing keel means she can navigate shallow water. It has a small diesel so you aren't depending on sails all the time. But listen to this; "Ancillary equipment includes four complete SCUBA sets, wet suits, weight belts, and a certified high pressure compressor with attachments for dual Hookah use. Also included is a ten Kilowatt dieselpowered generator. The main engine is a twenty-seven horsepower Yanmar diesel." he went back to reading the ad.

"You're going to buy a boat? "

"I didn't say I was going to buy it. But for a dive boat it is a dream come true. We could live on board and go anywhere we ever wanted to. Do you think you could live on a boat?" he asked.

"Well first of all you keep saying we. Does that mean you have decided we are a couple, you and I? Or have you someone else in mind?"

Hal was stunned. "Um, I guess I just jumped to the conclusion that we are a couple, or at least we will be, I hope."

Jan leaned back against the kitchen cupboard, her arms crossed in front of her. "I need a definition of couple. We still haven't decided where this relationship is headed. We've come to it sooner than I thought. So what would you think of moving in with me?"

Hal smiled, "It would save a lot of problems for sure." But we have to seal it with a kiss."

She came across the coach to him. They met in a deeply passionate embrace; Jan had tears in her eyes. "If you kiss me like that one more time we will be sealing it with more than a kiss."

He smiled, stroking her cheek, "Promises, promises, promises."

They ate supper in an unusually quiet mood, each

deep in thought. She was dishing up apple pie when she surprised him yet again.

"So how do we find out about this boat?" she asked "

I have a diving friend in Austin, I could call him and ask him to go have a look. If he says it looks good we can go check it out."

"But honey, you haven't even said how much this sailboat would cost. Can you, or we, even afford it? "

"They are asking thirty five thousand," he admitted. "But it sounds like a really good deal. We could even start a dive business, or take people on cruises."

Jan slumped into her spot on the couch, "But technically I am still in the army, and so are you. We both have to go back, and I only have a couple more weeks."

Hal folded the paper. "I'll tell you what, I'll call Jesse and get him to send a marine surveyor down to appraise the boat. Meanwhile we can start heading north. If the boat sounds good we can decide if we really want it. Otherwise we forget the boat and head back to Toronto. If you decide to take your release, fine, if not, well, we'll work it out. As far as affording it, I have almost enough back pay coming to pay cash for it. "

"Where could we go with it? And live aboard? What about cooking and washing, and eating?"

"A boat that size could sail around the world. As far as appliances and conveniences it will have at least as much as your motor home. Just think, crossing the Caribbean under sail power takes no fuel. Dropping anchor in a bay somewhere means no hotels or RV parks. We can work when we want, where we want, if we want."

"You make it sound so wonderfully easy. Do you really know how to handle a sail boat?"

"Honey I am not just a broken down diver. I also hold an instructors rating with the Royal Yachting Association, and I'm a licensed pilot. Yes I could handle that boat in my sleep."

Hal went to use the telephone in the campground office. He soon returned with a big smile.

"Jesse says he has to go to Galveston tomorrow anyway. He'll check it out and get back to us. Meanwhile, no matter what we are going to do about a boat, we need to head back to Toronto."

She had several questions when he returned. "So back up a bit. What is a Hookah rig? Isn't that the thing the Turkish men use to smoke opium and tobacco?"

Hal laughed, "I can see where our first outing will be a training cruise. Honey a Hookah is an airline from the boat to the diver so you don't have to wear a tank on your back. The only problem is the hose is only so long so you can't go very far or very deep."

Later they were poring over a map trying to decide what route they would take back to Texas.

"Hal, if we buy the boat, could we sail it down here? "

"Yes we certainly could. "

"Then instead of driving 1800 miles back to Texas, and another 2000 to Toronto. Why don't we fly to Galveston, check the boat, and then fly home? "

"Well my dear, remember the sticker they put on your windshield when you came into Mexico? That sticker is your guarantee that you will not leave your vehicle in Mexico. If you leave the country without the bus they'll charge you import taxes on it and a lot more. What we could do is leave the rigs in Galveston and fly home from there. "

"Yes, you're right. I had forgotten about that sticker business." Jan took another map out of a drawer. "So when do we leave and which way do we go?"

Hal stroked his chin, "Which way did you come down? We don't really want to cover the same roads twice. "

"I crossed the border at Nogales and came down through Hermosillo, Mazatlan, Acapulco, and Palenque to Chetumal." She explained.

"Okay so you have seen the west coast. We can go up the east coast on the new superhighway One-Eighty through Merida, and Hermosa and follow the coast north. We can spend a night at Vera Cruz, then up through Tampico, and Victoria to Texas at Reynosa. From Pharr we can take highway Fifty-Nine to Houston and then Interstate Forty-Five to Galveston. We can check out the boat then catch a direct flight to Toronto."

"Wow! That sounds easy when you say it. It would take me a week of map reading to figure all that out."

Hal scratched his head, deep in thought. "What size engine have you got in this bus?" he asked.

"Um, I think it's a four hundred horsepower diesel. Why? "

"Just a thought, but instead of driving both vehicles we could put a tow bar on my truck. Then we could share the driving, burn less fuel, and travel together." He offered.

"That sounds like a plan. When do we start? "

"First I have to find a shop that can put a hitch on the bus, and a tow bar on the truck." Hal leafed through a tourist service guide as he spoke.

Chapter Eighteen

The welder showed up early the next morning and by noon the truck and bus were connected and ready for the road. Hal took the first shift at the wheel.

Jan was driving when they reached Merida. When she spotted a Walmart, pulled in and parked.

"We need to go shopping Jan?"

"No, but we're only stopping overnight. I often park on Walmart lots. Look! Over there," she pointed. Several other RVs were also parked on the lot. After they had settled in Jan started to fix supper.

"Hal," she called. "I have an idea. What if we sell the coach and camper to pay for the boat? They will just sit all the time we're cruising anyway."

Hal just looked at her. He was almost speechless. He had not considered the possibility that she might share the cost of the boat. Now he was in a dilemma. They hadn't known each other that long and neither had discussed the future of their relationship.

"Well, we'll have to see." He mumbled. It was a weak reply but her suggestion was a complete surprise.

"Hal, just listen. You know I am a registered nurse. I am also a certified E. M. T. You mentioned something about selling cruises and dive trips. All we have to do is get me dive certified and we're a team. I mentioned that Dick and I had a boat so I am not totally green in that regard. You said the boat had all the equipment we would need, and it has three cabins so we could take two couples at once. The only thing I can think of is a good medical kit and maybe an A. E. D. What else could we possibly need except maybe a license?"

Hal sat back and stroked his chin. "So okay, I know what E. M. T. means, but what the hell is an A. E. D.? Then are you talking about a full blown business or a part time thing whenever we need to raise some money? As for me, I really don't want to spend all my time babysitting a bunch of seasick wannabe Jacque Cousteau types. I also want no part of being a party boat loaded with drunks, or a sex cruise barge."

Jan smiled, "I agree, we need to do it on as required basis to maintain our cash flow. As far as my training goes? Well as an Emergency Medical Technician I am qualified to work in an ambulance. I can give whatever emergency treatment is required to preserve life, stabilize a patient for transport. I can also administer medication and do minor surgery under the remote supervision of a doctor. The AED is an Automatic Electronic Defillibrator device used in the event of cardiac arrest, or heart attack. It replaces CPR. The medical kit is an advanced first aid kit and carries a variety of medications and tools for emergencies. If someone gets hurt at sea, or on a remote tropical island we need to be prepared. We should be able to set bones and do stitches. And just what do you mean no sex cruises? What about just the two of us? "

"Whoa." Laughed Hal. "We don't even know if we are going to buy this boat. Let's not get our hopes up. I'm still wondering about you selling your coach, I'm not sure that's such good idea. I'll tell you what. Let's look at the boat first, then before we decide for sure we need to get back to Toronto. I wasn't sure if I wanted to get out of the army or not, and I need to know what I am in for with my pension and back pay. Then you need to find out if you can get an early release, you said your current enlistment wasn't up for two more years. What if they won't release you? We're getting a bit carried away with our planning. I had just planned to buy the boat to live on and dive from. Now it is getting so complicated."

Jan sat back, toying with a pillow and staring out the window. It had seemed like such a good idea. Had she scared him off with her proposal? Had she fallen in love with this guy to the point that they were just going to automatically live together? Now she was going to worry. Maybe he didn't really want her around anymore. After meeting his ex-wife she could understand why he might be reluctant to get involved with another woman.

Suddenly the realization dawned on her; she was acting like a partner. For the first time the real possibility of them being married occurred to her. No wonder he was suddenly walking soft and backing up.

Hal kneaded the scar of his missing fingers. He had to find a way to slow Jan down without hurting her feelings. It just didn't seem right to him that she should sell this coach to buy him a boat. It would be like forming a partnership and it would be tough to get out of. They had grown so close in the past weeks. He wanted to be with her, to share his life with her, but holy crap! Was she hinting at getting married? The thought brought on an instant headache. He had been there and done that and sworn never again.

"Hey, cheer up Jan. There is a Senior Mac's restaurant. Lets go out for supper tonight."

Jan looked around the parking lot, "I don't see any restaurant." She replied. "Over there, under the golden arches."

She looked at him quizzically, "That's a McDonald's!

"Si senorita," Hal laughed, "Senior Mac's."

"Oh you, always trying to be funny." She had forgotten they were still in Mexico.

Hal reached for his foot and slid up his pant leg. "I haven't had a Big Mac fix for weeks." He said while attaching the prosthesis.

Jan rose and walked toward the bathroom, "Just let me fix my hair a bit." They were less than a block from the beach and the smell of the sea greeted them as they stepped outside. From somewhere close by came the strains of a Mariachi band playing 'Guantanamera'. Night had fallen and a slight breeze rustled through the palms as they walked across the parking lot. They picked up the pace as the smell of French fries and grilled meat intercepted them. Suddenly it was more enticing than all the tortillas and tamales in Mexico.

Inside there were few customers so there was no waiting. Jan ordered a McChicken sandwich combo and coke while Hal went for the Double Big Mac combo and a chocolate shake. He took the loaded tray to a table while Jan stopped for straws, ketchup, and napkins. They were soon too busy eating and enjoying to be bothered talking. The special sauce ran down Hal's chin and the chopped lettuce littered his empty sandwich box.

As he finished and wiped his face he took a long pull on the milkshake. "Mm-mm that was so good."

Jan, her mouth still full of chicken merely nodded in agreement.

Leaving the restaurant arm in arm Jan exclaimed, "Senior Mac's huh? It tasted like home cooking to me. I guess I needed a Mac fix also."

Hal woke in the morning with the previous day's conversation still in his head. The very thought of marriage scared him. He had to get Jan talking about it and let her know it was not in his plans for the future.

Jan was up and had made coffee when she saw him sit up. She pushed the button on the toaster knowing he would be out momentarily. "Good morning sleepy." She called.

Before long they were northbound on the coastal highway. Their next stop would be the coastal city of Vera Cruz. Then they had just one more long day of driving before they reached the U. S. border. Jan began seeing signs advertising fresh camarone along the highway. A vision of fresh boiled shrimp tempted her. Hal slept while she did her shift.

At the next open air roadside market she pulled in and stopped. Going quickly from booth to booth she soon had several bags full of purchases. Back in the coach she stored tomatoes, lettuce, green onions, and celery in the crisper. The seafood she divided into two bags. The first held one kilogram of the large fresh shrimp for supper. The second bag, containing two kilos went in the freezer. She drove back onto the highway. Hal had not budged. She had a surprise for him this evening. Senior Mac's indeed, she chuckled silently. Not on my shift, she promised.

Jan slowed the coach as they entered the outskirts of Vera Cruz. Hal was up sitting in the co-pilot's seat and studying a map. "Honey, turn right at the next traffic light."

She did as he directed and they soon arrived at a beautiful beach. She drove to the end of the pavement and stopped. Getting out to look around they disturbed a flock of wild Flamingos. Their great pink wings soon carried them down the beach to another spot.

The gulf was nearly calm, tiny wavelets murmured ashore on nearly white sand. Hal got them each a can of beer and unloaded the lawn chairs. Despite his afternoon nap he was tired. The long days on the road were worse than working.

As they sat and enjoyed the view Jan voiced a request. "When you find a spare minute would you mind gathering some wood and starting a fire?"

"Sure, any particular reason "

"Yes my dear, tonight I am making supper."

"You need a fire to make a peanut butter sandwich? "

"Oh you ass!" Jan threw a towel at him.

She finished her beer and went back inside. Through the windshield she could see Hal among the trees. He was hobbling around, limping more than usual. She busied herself making a salad from the fresh veggies. That done she put it in the fridge and retrieved the bag of giant shrimp. Taking each of them in turn she gave it a twist and deftly removed its head. Next she took two more beers out to where Hal was preparing a fire pit. She handed him a can and went to get her largest pot.

"We need this half full of water and then heat it to boiling." She instructed as she disappeared into the bus.

"Wow, how many eggs are you gonna hard boil?" he teased.

Hal soon had the fire going and the big pot on a grating above it.

Jan came out and poured a cupful of a spicy mixture into the water. "Crab boil!" She stated, in answer to his questioning glance.

"We've got crabs?" He teased.

"NO!" Said Jan, trying not to laugh, "I don't mean crotch crickets. I stopped today and bought some lovely jumbo shrimp."

"You stopped? I didn't know that. "

"Honey, there are a lot of things you don't know." They nursed their second can of beer until the water began to boil. Jan uncovered a large bowl and for the first time Hal saw the shrimp.

"Mm-mm nice ones."

Jan dumped the shrimp into the pot then retreated inside. "Twelve minutes," she called, "Then scoop them out and bring them inside."

She had prepared a vinaigrette dressing for the salad and some home made seafood sauce for the shellfish. "Peel and eat" She announced, "The only way to enjoy fresh shrimp."

She dumped a dozen pink shelled creatures on each plate and served them

Hal peeled the shell off the first one and dipped in it the sauce before taking a bite. "Mm-mm delicious." He reached for another. "What's in this sauce, it's great?"

"Just some ketchup, horseradish and hot sauce."

They ate in silence; the shrimp were soon gone followed by the salad. She finished it off with glasses of the leftover white wine. "Hal, I saw you limping today. Is the stump bothering you?

"Yeah, it is. It almost feels like a lump at the end. "

"You better let me have a look at it," she said, the concern apparent in her voice.

Hal moved to the couch and removed the plastic foot. The white stocking underneath had blood on it. Jan gently peeled back the covering. It took but a moment to discover the cause.

"Oh Hal, it is infected and it looks like an abscess next to the bone. I have some antibiotic here but we need to get you to a doctor."

"Well we'll be in the states tomorrow. We'll find a Veteran's Hospital and get it fixed up."

Jan leaned forward and sniffed the wound. I don't think there is any gangrene but you can't play around with infections in the tropics. Let me get you some pills then I'll do the dishes and get to bed early.

"Right," grinned Hal. "Bed, early, the best offer I've had all day."

Chapter Nineteen

Arriving at the Galveston harbor they found it bustling with activity. People were coming and going on the pier and several boats were moving toward the channel. A quick inquiry at the marina office gave them the location of the boat. The manager assured them the owner of the boat was not far away. They walked down the pier and out onto the floating docks.

Their destination was slip number three nine two. Circling seagulls screamed overhead, and music floated across the bay from a bar on the far side. They found the slip and for a moment just stared at the boat.

Hal walked to the end of the adjoining slip and checked her stern. In large black letters the name 'Sea Fever' was displayed above her home-port, 'Galveston, Texas'. For Hal it was love at first sight. The boat was spotless. The gear was stowed, and even the halyards were properly coiled and lashed to the mast. The deck was well rubbed teak. She did not appear to be forty feet long but Hal realized it was because she had such a broad beam.

"Hello there." Came a voice from behind them. "Can I help you?

"This your boat?"

"Yes it is! Is your name Hal Sigurdson?"

"That's me, and this is my lady friend Jan Northwaite. I take it you were talking to my pal Jesse?"

"Yes, he was here last week, nice fellow, knows his boats. "

"So may we go aboard?" Asked Hal.

"Be my guests, the cabin is unlocked. We can take her for a spin if you like, I'll be here on the pier."

Hal stepped aboard through a gap in the rail. Reaching back he offered Jan his hand to cross the gap. He eyeballed the hardware on deck, impressed with what he saw. He slid back the companionway hatch and looked below.

Jan saw the smile on his face and bent to look. She found it hard to believe what she was looking at. The interior cabins were done in dark polished woodwork. Red and gold velvet curtains covered the portholes. The upholstery was dark brown with white trim. The sun coming through the glass skylight kept everything bright and cheerful. Even the galley counter boasted a butcher-block top.

"Nice," said Hal, "Very nice." He motioned for Jan to go below and followed her. For several minutes they just looked around.

"Three separate cabins," noted Jan.

"She was built in 1985," said Hal. But she looks like a brand new boat. Look at the woodwork. Teak, mahogany, and holly everywhere, and the upholstery is perfect."

Jan stepped into the galley. "The fridge is alcohol electric and the stove is propane." She ran her hand over the butcher-block counter. "Honey I think I am in love. This is one gorgeous chunk of boat."

Hal stepped out of the engine room as Jan spoke. He had been snooping in cupboards, access panels, and lifting bilge grates. Several times he opened lockers and found the contents surprising to say the least. "That engine is spotless and you could eat off the floor in there."

A voice from the cockpit interrupted them as the

owner stepped aboard. "So did you find any problems, have questions. Did you find everything?"

Hal sat on a couch resting his aching foot. He felt another phantom pain from the missing appendage. "What about the sails? What shape are they in?"

The owner smiled, "We can hoist them if you like. There are seven of them, two mains, two jibs, a genoa, and two spinnakers. The oldest is about 5 years old. They are all in excellent condition. The owner of the sail loft at the marina will vouch for them."

"And Jesse said you had a report from a marine surveyor?"

"Right here in this drawer. All the ships papers, registration, ship's log, engine log, survey report and receipts for work done over the years." He opened a drawer in a mahogany and holly desk .

"OK," Answered Hal, "I'll look them over later. So what does she draw and what speeds can she make?"

"Her draft with the swing keel up is just over four feet. Keel down it is eight feet. The maximum on the diesel is about twelve knots and under sail alone she averages about eight knots. But if you get close hauled in a gale force she flies. We have hit eighteen knots."

Jan and Hal were having lunch at the marina when he spoke between bites." So? What did you think of Sea Fever?"

Jan smiled, "Dumb question! I'm no expert, but I sure liked what I saw. Living aboard her would be no hardship."

By nightfall they had made their decision, paid a deposit, and had the transfer paperwork filed. The Harbormaster agreed to let them leave the coach behind the marina and they had reservations on a flight to Toronto the next day.

* * * *

"So how was the diving?" Was the first question his doctor asked. Then without waiting for a reply he continued. "You were limping when you came in. How long has that been bothering you?"

"About a week or so," replied Hal. "My girl friend is a nurse and she gave me some antibiotic. She said it's abscessed but not gangrenous yet."

He was up on the stretcher and removing his foot.

"How about the rest of you? No aches or pains? "

"No." Said Hal but I do have a question.

"Well shoot." Ordered the physician.

"I have decided I want to go back to Civvy Street. How do I go about getting a medical release? And what about a pension and my back pay?

"The Veteran's Affairs office is just down the hall. They can get your answers and help you with paperwork."

Jan was waiting for him in the cafeteria. "How was it?" She asked.

"Well they cleaned it up, gave me a shot and a prescription and I am good to go. How about you?"

Jan smiled, "It will take a few days to arrange a release medical, get the paperwork done, and get my final pay but no problems. When they asked why I wanted a release so suddenly I told them I was had been diagnosed with Post Traumatic Stress Disorder. Which is true, no Problem. I was going to tell them I was pregnant but I didn't think that would work.

"You're what?" Hal's eyes grew wide.

"No silly, I'm not, not yet anyway."

Hal relaxed a bit. "Well anyway, my payout will more than cover the boat. And my pension will be almost enough to live on. Are you sure you want to be part of this crazy operation?"

She took his hand in hers, "In for a penny in for a pound."

Back at their hotel they worked on lists of things and supplies they would need on the boat. Jan looked after the food, medical, sleeping, and clothing side. Hal made notes for binoculars, engine spares, maps, and hardware. Suddenly he looked up.

"I know something that boat doesn't have.

"And what is that?" she asked.

"A dinghy! There is no tender, or lifeboat, or raft or anything. Without one we would have to swim if we wanted to go ashore on a beach." He added the item to his growing list. "Of course it would also be handy if something happens to the boat."

Three days later they were trying to relax in the Toronto airport lounge. Bad weather farther west had delayed the arrival of their flight. The result was a late arrival back in Galveston. The sun had already set and there was a smell of rain in the air.

At the airport parking lot, Hal unlocked the truck. "Lets just grab a hotel and go down to the marina tomorrow.

"That sounds like a plan," sighed Jan. "It's been a long day.

"Hey Jan, do you want to go out for dinner?

"Sure hon.

"Great, because I saw a hot-dog cart on the corner."

She glared at him, and laughed at the same time. "Okay, you got me. You bugger."

The Gulf Winds Motel sign led them to a parking lot only a block from the marina. As they retrieved their suitcases Jan noticed a restaurant next door. "It's not exactly a hot-dog stand, but it says they do have a buffet."

Hal still favored his bad leg. Limping as they approached the lobby he stopped to rest for a moment.

"I can see it's really hurting again." She observed. "When we get settled in I'll get you your pills." She watched him fill out the room registration card. He got a loving poke in the ribs when she saw him enter their names as Mister and Mrs. H. Sigurdson.

"Now I wonder if he is just practicing or if that is a hint." She thought. After taking their suitcases to the room she slipped out to the truck and brought in his crutches.

"I don't need those damned things," He exploded.

"But dear, if you don't stay off it and let it heal how will you manage to get around on the boat?"

He reluctantly agreed, and removed the foot. "Next thing I know you will be buying me a deck chair with wheels." He grumbled.

In the restaurant Jan voiced a suggestion. "You need to stay off that foot. Do you want to order from the menu, or shall I go and fix a plate and surprise you?"

"Well I haven't had a surprise for days, go for it." She surprised him with the size of the plate she brought back and the variety of food she had stacked up on it.

"Wow!" Was all he could say.

"Well growing boys need to eat to get their strength back." She quipped.

"Honey, that's not what makes my boy grow, and you know it."

Jan blushed, "Hal, people can hear you." She whispered .

"Okay, but I hope you don't get seasick when we rock the boat."

She popped a shrimp into his mouth to shut him up.

Chapter Twenty

A light chop in the bay threw sparkling wavelets against the boat as the purring diesel took them slowly out of the harbor Jan spread a blanket on the deck and relaxed. Hal admired her new bikini, its tiny design could be described as barely legal. It distracted him from his study of the boat's behavior. He had also changed to a new swimsuit.

Through dark tinted sunglasses Jan admired his tanned and muscular body. She had become so used to his scars that she rarely noticed them anymore.

They had cleared the harbor and the Intercoastal Waterway when Hal shut down the diesel. It took but a moment to raise the main sail and unfurl the small jib sail on the bow. As he tightened the main winch the sails filled with wind and Sea Fever moved forward with the silent power. He swung the helm and changed course to due south, away from the coast. The boat cut through the water smoothly, leaving barely a ripple behind. After engaging the autopilot Hal slipped out of his swimsuit and took a beer from the cockpit fridge.

"Would you like a beer or something honey?" he called to Jan.

She sat up and returned her glance to him. Seeing him naked she smiled and rose, walking to the cockpit.

"A beer would be nice." She smiled as she slipped the bikini top off over her head. She shook her head to let the wind blow her long hair over her shoulder.

Hal was frozen with delight as he admired her perfect breasts. The chill of the wind had already hardened her nipples. She smiled, pirouetted on the teak deck, and then slowly slid the bikini bottoms to the wood at her feet.

"You like?' She asked teasingly, knowing Hal was admiring her every curve and cranny. She reached and took the offered beer.

"It sure is different than driving down the highway."

The electronic steering device had the boat under control as Hal stepped toward her. "God, you're a beautiful woman," he whispered. His voice husky with the desire he was feeling. He took her in his arms and kissed her. His chest to her breasts, his erect manhood pressed to her tummy. She tangled her tongue around his, returning his passion.

She reached down and grasped his hardened member, "I think this guy likes me too."

He pushed her back against the cabin wall and stroked her swollen mound. They were touching and exploring each other in a sexually induced state of lust when Hal suddenly pulled back.

"Son of a bitch," he called, looking upward.

Jan heard the beating sound of the approaching helicopter before she saw it.

The pilot waved as he passed close by, then circled the boat and continued on his way.

"Well I hope the bastard got a good look," he said.

"Oh honey, we were so close together he couldn't see much any way, except maybe your bare ass."

The passion of the moment had cooled and they each went back to their forgotten beer.

Hal, satisfied with the operation of the autopilot, changed course and headed north again. The low profile of Padre Island soon came into view. He checked a map and the GPS and changed course slightly. Jan came and sat beside him.

"So how do you like her?" He asked.

"I love it, except for helicopters. Where are we going?"

Hal pointed to the map. "There is a little bay on the shoreward side of the island. It looks well protected and well off the beaten track. I thought we might spend the night there."

Hal cranked up the keel at the entrance to the shallow bay then lowered the mainsail while Jan went forward and furled the jib. At his instruction she released the bow anchor.

She jumped back as it splashed into the azure water and splashed cool seawater on her naked chest.

"Oh!" She gasped, "It's cold."

As she stepped down into the cockpit Hal took her hand and led her below. He pressed her back on the berth in the master stateroom. No helicopter jockey would interrupt them here. Moving over her he kissed her with pent-up passion.

She moaned as he moved to her throat and nuzzled her ears. She raised her hands to his shoulders as he slid down to her breasts. First one, then the other he sucked and licked her matching twins.

Jan was breathing fast and deep, knowing what was to come but wanting what he was doing.

His swirling tongue poked her navel before continuing across her stomach. His nose poked through her pubic hair and found the protruding tip of her swollen and sensitive clitoris.

She gasped as he took the miniature erection in his lips, sucking gently before flicking his tongue across it. She spread her legs wide as he continued down, his searching tongue licking and poking in her most tender spots. She felt his erection on her leg, the dampness of his pre-cum leaving a wet trail. She wanted to take that rigid mast into her mouth, but she also wanted it as far into her as it would go.

Hal paused and took a condom from the bedside table. She took it from him and rolled it down over his rock hard love tool. He raised her legs, her thighs on her chest and her feet hooked over his shoulders as he lowered himself to fill her aching womanhood. Slowly, gently he buried himself in her waiting crevice. The familiar feel of soft oiled velvet encased him as her wanton vaginal juices flowed around him.

He had no sooner rubbed her clit with his pelvis than the first orgasm surprised her. He felt the clenching muscles grasp him as be began the rhythmic motions they both enjoyed. The swinging skin sack containing his testicles bumped against her lower opening as he pulled back and thrust, again and again.

With her legs over his shoulders she was pinned down, unable to move. She lowered her legs to the bed and thrust upwards. Her hands moved to his lower back and pulled him in deeper.

Hal rose up and looked into her eyes, "I think we are rocking the boat."

They both laughed and continued their plunging actions. Jan grabbed his shoulders,

"Yes, baby oh Yes, Bingo! Oh Hal don't stop, oh just don't stop!" A tremendous orgasm wracked her entire body; she froze for a moment, unable to move.

He felt her contractions increase, her muscles pumping him of their own accord. He moved faster, taking long strokes, almost leaving her throbbing vagina then slamming back into her, burying his entire length. In seconds the combination of their muscles brought him to a mind-blowing orgasm. He came as she came, emptying his store of semen in an exquisite series of contractions of his own muscles.

After a long moment the pulsations ended. Both panted, short of breath from the exertions. He remained over her, his penis slowly losing its hardness while each enjoyed the after effects of a wonderful coupling.

Hal lowered his lips to hers, giving her a tender kiss. "I love you babe.

"And I love you too." She whispered, her body still tingling from his skillful attention to her needs.

"I think I need a swim," said Hal. "I seem to be all sweaty and sticky." He left the bed, and limped up to deck. She heard the splash as he went over the side.

A moment later a second splash echoed across the bay. As she broke the surface following her dive she shouted. "Me too! Can you still go three for three?"

He swam to her and they treaded water as they embraced. Already she felt him growing against her leg.

"What do you think?" he asked.

She smiled and giggled, the blue-green water washing over her uplifted breasts   " Promises, promises, promises."

Chapter Twenty-one

"Paul? Paul Donelly?" Hal gaped in wonder as he faced the man in the dive shop.

"Hal Sigurdson, well I'll be damned, what's an old wreck rat like you doing in Galveston?"

What started out as a handshake became a hug as the two old friends greeted each other.

"Me? What about you? Last I heard you were diving on a wrecked steamer in the Suez Canal with a Canadian Army dive team."

"Yeah, well some gyppo with an AK-47 put a round in my chest. That ended my army diving. So I bought this place. "

"But what happened to you? I heard you got killed in 'Stan."

"Not quite." Replied Hal. "I lost some fingers and a foot to a grenade." He held up his hand.

"Well hey enough war stories. Who is the beautiful lady you brought along?"

"Honey, this is Paul Donelly. He and I trained together and did a lot of diving together years ago. Paul this is Jan Northwaite. She was a nurse in 'Stan and looked after me when they flew me out on a Med-Evac transport. I found her last month in Mexico of all places."

Paul extended his hand. "Well Jan, I am sure as hell glad to meet you, and the pleasure is all mine. Now what can I do for you two?"

"Hal has been teaching me to dive, I need to get

tested and certified. We're thinking of running dive cruises on our boat."

Paul glanced at Hal and shrugged his shoulders.

"Yes," answered Hal to the invisible question. "I have been teaching her. She started on snorkel and has done a little SCUBA work. She knows the dive tables, decompression rules, nitrogen narcosis and a bunch of other stuff. I think she is ready."

"Well Hal old buddy, if you taught her she got the best training available. I just need her to write the test and get her a PADI card. Step into my office."

Jan was surveying the shop. There were stuffed fish, antique diving suits, spear guns, and all sorts of dive related equipment on display. In the office she sat at a desk and Paul handed her several sheets of paper. It took her less than an hour to complete the multiple-choice questions. At the bottom of the last was a certificate of diving proficiency to be signed by her examiner.

"Hal, you trained her so I can't sign her off. You are still PADI certified as instructor, right?"

"Yes, I am, do you need to see my card?"

"Hey no way man! You certified me. Remember?
"

"So have you ever heard of a dive boat named Sea Fever? "

"Hell yes." Said Paul. I have been servicing her gear for years. Why?"

"Well we bought her. I was concerned about when the compressor and tanks were last certified."

"Worry no more buddy. The annuals were done last month. If you want to use Nitrox the diaphragms are good for at least another ten years." He took a paper out of the printer, trimmed it, signed it, and laminated it in plastic. "There you go Jan." he said, shaking her hand. "Congratulations and welcome to the Brotherhood of Undersea Divers, That's BUD for short because we never dive alone."

Jan admired the card; the background was a diver silhouette against the red and white flag signifying 'Diver Down. ' "OK, but what the hell is this PADI you guys keep saying?"

Paul laughed at her request, "It stands for 'Professional Association of Diving Instructors' and it just means that you are certified by a couple of the best men to ever suck air from a tank. And you can dive with me anytime and anywhere."

Jan smiled at the compliment; he and Hal were like two peas in a pod.

"So if you guys are looking for customers I can pass the word." Offered Paul.

"Give us some time," said Hal. "We have a lot of details to work out first."

While preparing for their trip Hal purchased a small used rowboat for a tender. Then they bought a computer and a satellite phone. The pantry, freezer and fridges were stocked with food and they were good to go. At sunup the next morning they cast off. Their course took them Southward, for the beaches where they met.

Running under sails alone they were eleven days at sea along the Mexican coast before reaching the harbor at Playa Del Carmen. They serviced the boat, did some shopping and turned south once more. That afternoon they dropped anchor in the bay they had left the month before.

This was much deeper water than where they snorkeled the reef. Jan was anxious to strap on a tank and explore the new depths. Hal pulled out the gear and Jan began to don the required items. She noticed Hal staring at her.

"What?" She demanded.

Hal smiled at her and stripped off his shorts.

"Oh you." She laughed, but she stripped off her

bikini.

They descended together to the reef below. At first her attention was drawn by the colder water, she didn't see the color change. She also didn't need to look down to see if her nipples were hardening.

As they swam deeper the blue of the water caught her attention. This was her first SCUBA dive in tropical waters. It was like her first time snorkeling only better. There were more varieties of fish, coral and plants on the deeper reef. Tiny fishes in ornate colors swam among the plants, while larger ones patrolled the perimeter. She had just rounded a projection of coral when she felt Hal's hand on her thigh.

Their first sub sea kiss was awkward while wearing face-masks and mouthpieces. They would soon learn alternate methods. They removed the air tanks and laid them on the bottom. Their weight belts held them down.

Nearly floating in neutral buoyancy it was difficult to make the connection. Jan put her legs around Hal's hips and pulled. He slipped in without difficulty. He had to put his hands on her hips to pull and push her back and forth. Their heavy breathing produced dual streams of silver bubbles rising to the surface. The coupling was short lasted.

Jan began to giggle, and then laugh. Her facemask flooded and she lost her mouthpiece. Suddenly Hal was serious. He helped her with the airline while she cleared the mask. They strapped on the tanks and began the ascent to the surface. Jan was still laughing and coughing as she climbed the stern ladder to Sea Fever's deck.

"Whoa," she gasped between coughs, "Next time lets use the HOOKAH hose in shallow water. I damned near drowned. "

"Next time?" He replied. "You're a devil for

punishment."

"Well," She snickered, "At least you try to keep your promises." She toweled the salt water from her hair and continued downward across her still erect nipples.

Hal stowed their gear before reaching for a towel. As he dried he cocked his head to the breeze. There were no boats or vehicles in sight but he could hear the sound of an engine.

"What's the matter?" Asked Jan. She stood in the cockpit enjoying the sun while brushing her hair.

"Can you hear that engine?" Asked Hal. "It sounds like there may be a boat coming along the coast outside the bay."

Jan turned her head this way and that. "No, I don't hear it."

"Oh well, it doesn't really matter. I just thought it strange, maybe it's the big white yacht we saw the last time we were here. But it is getting louder, like it is coming this way. It might be wise to put some clothes on."

Hal wriggled into his swimsuit then pulled a tee shirt over his head.

"Yes, we wouldn't want to shock the neighbors. We would be the talk of the marina at Playa del Carmen tonight."

She went below and slipped into a light cotton shift. It covered her nudity, but just.

"Honey would you bring me a beer when you come up please?" Hal sat down on the bench seat near the helm.

The wind had veered to the south and some puffy cumulus clouds were forming out to sea. The long spit of land that formed the bay protected them from the wind and waves coming across the Caribbean. Jan appeared in the companionway hatch and handed Hal a can of beer. The moist sea air soon formed beads of sparkling perspiration on the cold can.

"Thank you dear." He offered as he ripped open the zip tab. He took a long pull at the can, enjoying the cold bitter taste of the lager. "Do you have any plans for supper?"

Jan pointed to a box in the corner of the cockpit. "If you set up that barbecue you bought I could take a couple of steaks from the freezer. We have veggies for a salad to go with it. "

"Sounds good to me." He took another swig of beer then turned and looked toward the entrance to the bay. An increase in the distant engine noise had caught his attention. A moment later a boat came into view, entering the bay. Hal picked up the binoculars to get a better look.

It was an old beat up shrimp boat. It's once white painted hull was stained with rust and black marks from the old tires hanging along the sides. The long wooden booms for towing the shrimp nets were tied back in the traveling position. These guys were not after shrimp. Besides the bay was too shallow for the shellfish community.

Hal suddenly stood and braced himself for a better look. Several of the crew of the approaching boat looked familiar. He felt a familiar chill run up his back. A feeling he had felt before, in combat, in Afghanistan.

"Honey!" He shouted. "You stay below, don't come up no matter what happens."

Jan replied, a touch of fear in her voice. "Why? What is it!"

"I think your shrimper friends just came to say hello." Hal slowly bent and opened the top cover of the port side cockpit bench. From a watertight case he withdrew a C-7 assault rifle. Slamming a loaded magazine into the gun he cycled the action. Now with a round in the chamber only the safety and a trigger pull were needed to fire. Deciding to utilize all the firepower he had, he attached an M-203 grenade launcher to the rifle. Lastly he loaded a 40MM high explosive grenade. If these cowboys wanted trouble he would hand it out. Wholesale!"

Chapter Twenty-Two

From her seat in the galley Jan could see Hal in the cockpit. She could not believe it when the C-7 suddenly appeared. She had no idea it was on board or from where it had come.

Hal sat near the helm. The weapon, unseen by the approaching Mexicans, lay on his lap. The other boat was straight ahead of Sea Fever and pointed right at them. It looked like they intended to come alongside. As it drew nearer a plume of black smoke from the exhaust accompanied by a roar from the engine and a white froth from the propeller indicated it had reversed the prop. It now drifted just ahead of the sailboat.

"Hey amigo," came the first voice. "You got some cervesa, maybe some whiskey for us?"

Jan was near shock. It was the same voice she first heard when the gang had tried to rape her. "Hal, its them." She whispered loudly.

"Yes, I know," he said. "Stay down."

"Amigo, you got a nice boat. I like to come and look inside, si?"

Again Hal said nothing.

The shrimper that had been talking walked forward to the bow and leaned over. When he straightened he had a shotgun in his hand. He proudly leaned the gun over his shoulder.

"Amigo, I think now I come on your boat." The old shrimp boat started moving forward.

Hal placed the fire selector in the three round burst position. He stood, pointed the rifle towards the shrimp boat and fired.

Instantly three white geysers erupted in the water right in front of the older boat. He raised the muzzle and aimed it at the shot gunners middle. He also watched the rest of the crew. Another gun appeared in the cabin doorway and swung around to point his way. Hal touched the trigger again.

This time the three 5. 56mm slugs tore through the woodwork beside the door. The gun fell to the deck, followed by its owner.

On the bow a foolhardy move by the first speaker became his last. He brought the shotgun down off of his shoulder and pumped a shell into the breach. He was just bringing it bear on Hal when three more light caliber bullets crossed the gap. They took the gunman in the chest. In the wheelhouse the Captain decided it was time to leave. The engine roared, smoke billowed from the exhaust and again the water foamed under the stern. The wheel was hard over as he attempted to escape this well armed and deadly sailboat.

Hal had twenty-four rounds left in the thirty round magazine. Judging where the engine would be he fired four more three round bursts. He put six rounds through the deck, and six more through the hull. He hoped to disable the engine and prevent the escape. The engine continued to roar. Hal put six more bullets through the deck below the exhaust stack. He was down to six bullets if the crew brought up another weapon

."Well shit!" he shouted, switching to the grenade launcher. He knew the 40MM explosive would just about blow the boat out of the water and kill the remaining crew but they had their chance.

"Not on my watch!" Jan heard him mumble as he switched the fire selector. Just as he angled the barrel up to fire the grenade there came a series of rattles and squeals from the big diesel engine. Then it died and all was silent except the waves slapping against Sea Fever's side.

Hal directed the rifle back to the wheelhouse. "All of you, out on deck, now!" he ordered. "If I see another gun, you all die."

Three remaining crewmen, including the Captain in his wheelchair, came out into the sunlight.

"It is you! You bastard gringo! I should have killed you the first time." Came the voice of the man in the chair.

"Not in the best day in your life." Shouted Hal. "Now you send one man forward to drop the anchor. If he touches a gun, I fire the grenade. Comprendez?"

Moments later the rattle of an anchor chain going out broke the silence of the bay. The birds and monkeys, quieted by the gunfire, now resumed their cheerful chatter. Hal called for Jan to come on deck.

"Honey, get on the radio phone and call the coast guard at Playa del Carman. Tell them we are being attacked by pirates and require immediate assistance."

"But Hal, isn't it all over?" Protested Jan.

"Well hell yes, but they don't know that. It will just make them respond faster Tell them we are in Bahia de la Ascension."

Jan carried out the instructions as Hal watched the third crewman return to the stern.

The shrimpers were wide eyed as they realized who Jan was. They had been lucky to escape jail the first time. This time they would be lucky if they did not face a death penalty.

In what amounted to an unnecessary display of force, Hal loaded a fresh magazine into the rifle and checked the loaded grenade. Going against that kind of firepower either barehanded or with a shotgun loaded with bird shot amounted to no more than a death wish.

By late afternoon the Mexican Coast Guard arrived in a high-speed cutter. It flashed through the bay entrance at full speed, spray going everywhere. On the bow a crewman manned a deck gun. The afterdeck held a boarding party armed to the teeth with assault rifles. They circled the anchored craft before slowing down. After realizing Hal had it under control and seeing the smoke pouring from the diesel they came along side.

Knowing his weapon was highly illegal in Mexico Hal discreetly slipped it under the seat.

A few moments later an officer stepped aboard from the cutter. He smiled and pointed at the seat concealing the C-7. "Of course if you are not on land you have not actually brought it into Mexico." He then looked up at the Canadian flag flying from the masthead. "Canada, a wonderful country, I hope to go there some day. But for now my friend we need you for the problem of paperwork. If you could come aboard the cutter it will save you the voyage to my office. I think it would take two or three days to get there. Si?"

Jan and Hal were on the coast guard ship for nearly an hour when the Captain rose and said, "So, it is enough. These banditos have been in trouble many times. This time I think it will be the last. In Mexico we still hang pirates."

The cutter crew had taken the others prisoner and put a man on the shrimpers boat. They rigged a towline and soon the pair of them steamed out of sight. Jan had disappeared into the galley but soon emerged on deck. She handed Hal a tall glass of dark brown liquid.

"A Cuba Libre." She said. "With a lot of Cuba and a little libre and a shot of lemon. I think you need to 'splice the mainbrace."

Hal took a swallow and nearly choked. "Holy shit woman!" What the hell is that? And what is this mainbrace thing?"

"It is three shots of dark rum, three shots of coke, a dash of lemon and one ice cube." I read a book once where British sailors getting their daily ration of rum would say it was time to "Splice the Mainbrace."

"Well if it isn't too much trouble do you think you could put some more libre in my Cuba before I fall overboard?" He set aside the glass before tackling the task of assembling the new barbecue. Before long it hung on the ship's rail where it was supposed to be. He sat back to admire his work and finish his drink.

"Very nice dear," commented Jan. But I don't recall buying any charcoal." "That's because we didn't."

"And so what do we cook the steaks with?"

"Oh ye of little faith my sexy nursy friend, behold!" Hal opened a little cupboard below the helm and produced a large bag of charcoal and a bottle of lighter fluid. "Left behind by the previous tenants." He smiled.

.Jan went below to prepare the steak while Hal lit the barbecue. After that he took out the C-7, unloaded it, cleaned it, and put it back in the watertight bag.

"Thanks Jesse," He whispered. Knowing his friend had put the Canadian army issue rifle aboard. Had the original owner left it, he had no doubt it would have been the similar American model M-16 rifle.

Jan came up the companionway. "Honey can we go somewhere else tomorrow, I just don't feel right around here anymore.

Hal had a thought. They were not that far from the New River in Belize. Maybe they should cruise through the jungle on the river instead of all this coastal stuff. It would be good to get out of salt water for a while.

Chapter Twenty-Three

Jan relaxed on the forward deck as they sailed south along the coast. She loved listening to the hiss as the bow of Sea Fever cut through the nearly turquoise waters of the Caribbean. The wind was light but steady. The halyards and stays whistled slightly in the wind. Her tan had darkened to the point where she rarely bothered using suntan lotion. They were close to a populated coast and often passed other boats so a brief bikini hid her usual nudity.

Hal leaned on the wheel enjoying the view during his shift. At times he actually looked at something other than the beauty on the foredeck. In the distance the southern most point of Mexico came into view.

As they rounded the point near Ambergris Cay and entered Bahia de Chetumal he set a course for the town of Corozal. They needed to stop there to clear customs into Belize.

Alongside the channel lay the barrier reef. He was looking forward to touring this unique spot with Jan.

"Honey, would you furl the jib and drop the main please. We'll use the diesel to come alongside the customs wharf."

Jan jumped to do as she was bid and Hal started the diesel engine. Before long they were tying up at the official dock between the harbormasters office and the Belize Port of Entry office.

"Good afternoon folks, welcome to Belize." Came a call from dockside.

Hal turned off the engine and stepped off the boat to secure the stern mooring line. He was surprised at being greeted in English, having forgotten that Belize was English speaking.

"Yes sir," replied Hal. "We need to clear customs and take on some supplies then we will head for the New River."

Jan handed their passports up from below and Hal transferred them to the officer. After a quick glance he handed them back. "Will you be staying in Belize for long?"

"Just a few days. We would like to go upriver and visit the Lamani Mayan Site." Answered Hal.

The customs officer looked up at their towering mast. "I don't know if you can get under the bridge at Orange Walk. You may have to get a ride on a charter boat."

Hal had not considered the possibility of a low bridge. Perhaps a day trip on a charter would be easier than sailing fifty miles up the river. "Okay, thanks. Now is there a place we can pick up a few groceries?"

The officer pointed at an alley between the two government buildings. "If you go through there it will take you to a market. They should have anything you need."

By mid-afternoon they were approaching Orange Walk. Already the trip had proven interesting. Besides the monkeys and tropical birds they had seen several large snakes and a few crocodiles. Hal had raised the swing keel and kept an eye on the depth finder. There were numerous sandbars and shallows and the river channel was not well marked.

Jan was sitting on the cockpit bench reading a guidebook she had picked up at the market. She had just described the local town when Hal interrupted her.

"Oh damn, look at that." he pointed ahead.

A low bridge carried the highway over the river blocking their passage. Throttling back the engine he turned toward a dock with several tour boats. On the pier a young man appeared and took the line thrown by Jan.

"I guess this is as far as we go." Said Hal as he stepped ashore and secured the stern line.

The dark skinned fellow smiled a toothless grin and replied. "It sure is! Unless you want to either cut the mast or capsize the boat."

"Not today, thank you. But who do we talk to about a charter?"

The man scratched his head. He wore ragged blue jeans, bare feet and a tattered shirt. "You can talk to one of the boat Captains but I can tell you as much as they can." He pointed at a large jet boat tied to another dock. "You can charter a boat just for yourselves, or you can take a scheduled trip on a regular boat. Either way you don't want to leave until tomorrow if you are going to Lamani."

The early morning air was cool and brisk at the speed the big jet boat traveled upstream. The coffee colored waters of the winding river cut through the jungle on a meandering course. The Captain often slowed or stopped to show the passengers points of interest. It took nearly an hour to cover the twenty-two miles. Even with twenty-five people aboard the boat was remarkably quick and agile.

Arriving at a rickety dock, the waiting crew tied the lines and the passengers went ashore. Hal and Jan hung back, wanting to photograph much of the scenery. They followed a young lady in a white uniform as she led them through the jungle. The trail was not wide and several times Hal had to duck under low branches. The sun had warmed the air but it was pleasant in the shade of the big trees.

Before long they came to a clearing and the group

stopped. There was silence for a moment as everyone took in the view. Before them, surrounded by tall thick jungle, was a huge stone structure. The two sailors were awestruck. The size and complexity of the temple was far beyond anything they had imagined.

The guide stepped up on a rock to speak to the group. Her white outfit a stark contrast against the gray and black stone behind her. "Welcome to Lamani." She began. "This temple is named in the Mayan language and Lamani means 'submerged crocodile'. We believe the construction of this temple began in 1350 BC and continued until the inhabitants left it about 1650 AD. Its size is because with each succeeding ruler a new temple was built on top of the existing one."

The litany of the temple continued for some time. From the jungle around them came the screeches of the familiar howler monkeys, hundreds of bird species, and probably several animals. Jan pointed to a nearby tree where a toucan was preening its feathers. The bird's large green beak seemed larger than its black and white body.

The temple was as huge as it was amazing. Although it rose nearly one hundred feet, some of the trees of the rain forest still dwarfed it.

Jan read more from her guidebook. "It was located in 1917 but not excavated until 1974."

They explored the lower levels but Hal didn't want to climb the massive staircase because of his foot. "You go ahead. I'll wait here."

"No, I don't think so. Who will look after you if I fall or get stuck up there?"

At noon the group gathered in the shade for a box lunch provided by the Captain of their boat. Afterward they had two hours to wander the area before the boat ride back to Orange Walk.

They arrived back at the dock just before sunset. Hal waited until everyone had disembarked before approaching the Captain. "Would there be any problem with us staying tied up here overnight?" He asked.

"Not at all." Came the reply. "And there is a little restaurant and bar just across the way."

Back aboard Jan was preparing to start the evening meal. Hal took out the phone and checked for messages. There was a note from Paul at the dive shop in Galveston.

"Hey you two, where are you? If you haven't wrecked that boat yet, I have a couple looking for a dive cruise. I told them it might cost $750 per day but it would be all-inclusive. They are talking maybe ten days. They will fly to the closest port to meet you. Let me know when you can.

Paul "

Hal read it again then read it out loud for Jan. "That would be "$7500 for ten days of company? Sounds like good money to me."

Jan whistled, "Yes, but I wonder what they're like. Ten days is a long time on a boat with someone you can't stand. "

"Well we make them an offer. They pay half the money as a deposit, the other half before we sail. We meet them ashore and see if we all get along. If we don't like them the deal is off. And we have the option to put them ashore if things get out of hand."

Jan nodded. "Yes, but we better have that on paper. It's a lot of money without some kind of contract."

Hal laughed, "Do you think we can stay dressed and behave ourselves for ten days?"

Jan blushed, "We can always send them diving or shopping for a couple of hours. Which reminds me, we better get Paul to make sure they are PADI certified."

"Okay so where will we meet them? How soon? And what groceries will we need?" Hal bent to check the beer locker. His head was clicking over figures. At two cruises a month for ten months, that would bring in $150,000.

He opened a beer and sat back to think about it. In a couple of years they could buy a much bigger boat. Jan stroked his thigh very suggestively.

"Honey, if we have to behave for ten days maybe we should start storing up on sex before we meet these people."

Chapter Twenty-Four

They were still discussing details when they climbed into bed. Hal had gotten into a habit of lifting the sheet to admire Jan's nudity before shutting off the light. She rolled to him for a good night kiss, her hand finding and closing on an erect staff. His hand in turn found her waiting mound, his fingers parting her curly hair.

"Is this one to put in storage?" She whispered.

Though it was darker than the inside of a coalmine they had no trouble joining their bodies. Like an itch that demanded scratching they found each other. The chills and tingling of apprehension turned to hot flashes of satisfaction as their organs grew super-sensitive. In the heat of their passion they became almost animalistic. Their only thought centered on their coupling. In answer to natures design they fulfilled the act of procreation as it has been done since the beginning of time. Whether it be termed desire, lust, hunger or love they sated each other's need.

As with all nature's creatures from Aardvark to Zebra the desires were quenched and the need to mate consummated. A final kiss and each settled in for a good night's sleep. Hardly a moment had passed when Hal spoke.

"Um honey, we may have a problem!

"What is it Hal?

"Well, its like, I forgot the condom!"

The silence in the cabin reigned supreme for several seconds, only to be broken by Jan's nervous laugh. "Well maybe we just put something in storage."

Hal took her in his arms. "I am sorry Jan, it was stupid and careless, like a dumb teenager."

"Hey, I started it, remember? Don't panic, it might not be one of my fertile days. If it is, and I am, then we'll handle it." She kissed him again. "I love you."

"And I love you too."

A long time passed before they each fell into a restless slumber. With morning came a steady yet gentle rain. Hal grabbed a bar of soap and went up to the cockpit. An early morning shower in the rain was a great way to start the day. It also saved on their water supply.

Jan's head appeared in the companionway. Her hair was tousled, her eyes still looked sleepy. "Why didn't you tell me you were going for a shower?" Within minutes she too was soaping up, sharing the deck space.

A moment later, as if on command, a thundering deluge descended from the heavens. Then it stopped.

"Perfect timing," laughed Hal, "And a great rinse."

Jan was squeezing the excess water from her hair. The cool morning breeze raised goose bumps on her skin. Her nipples stood proud and erect. Hal admired the view, smiling and adoring.

"Its not fair," whined Jan in an artificially high voice.

"What isn't fair?

"Why do mine stand up when they get cold, and yours shrivels up?"

Hal burst out laughing. "It is something to do with protecting the sperm by keeping it warm. ."

Jan screeched with laughter. "Then the next time

you forget a condom I'll put an ice pack on you and freeze the little buggers.

"Then maybe we should keep a freezy pop in the fridge to put in you afterward. A post-coital contraceptive for horny nurses."

She threw the wet towel at him and went below. Hal was toying with his breakfast when Jan came to sit beside him.

"What's the matter honey? Don't want your eggs?"

"No they are great, I was just deep in thought "

"About this cruise no doubt?"

He drank some coffee then scooped up some egg. She waited while he finished eating, and then took his plate to the galley. He would talk about it when he had considered it for a while. Meanwhile she cleaned up the breakfast dishes and began to brush her hair.

Hal stood in the companionway and stared upriver. "I guess if we're going to do this we had better let Paul know. He needs to find out when they can leave and where they want to go. Then we have to decide where to meet them and how soon we can get there. All of a sudden it's getting complicated."

* * * *

Three days later they were tying up to the main pier at Belize City. It was nearly seventy miles from Orange Walk but it was the closest city with air service and a decent harbor Their guests were due to arrive by late afternoon so they spent some time getting the boat in top shape.

It was five o'clock and the sun was about to set when a rickety old taxi pulled up on the pier. From it climbed a tall dark man in his forties and a younger redheaded woman that Hal thought to be in her early thirties.

Hal stepped ashore." Might you be Tom and Kate?"

The man turned, "That would be us, and might you be the Captain of the Sea Fever"?

"I am he," said Hal, surprised at being called Captain for the first time. "Harold Sigurdson, But friends call me Hal. This is my First Mate Janice Northwaite, but she prefers Jan."Hal offered his hand.

"Tom Wakeman," came the reply as they shook hands, "and my wife Kate."

The driver had unloaded their bags and stood waiting. Tom paid him and they all turned to the boat.

"Nice!" Stated Tom as he stepped into the cockpit. "It's and older C and C isn't it? About forty feet?"

Again Hal was taken by surprise. "Yep, built in eighty-five." There was a note of pride in his voice. He hadn't expected his first cruise to be anyone that knew anything about boats.

"If you would leave your luggage in the cockpit we need to discuss a few things before we go any farther. If we all understand each other and know the rules it should prevent any troubles later on. We have of course a contract for you to read and sign but it is pretty basic. The first rule is, my word is law."

He let that sink in a moment. Jan handed them each a copy of the contract. The four were silent while the Wakeman's read. "Well it looks good to me. We aren't drinkers or party people. We just want to do some diving where the sea isn't congested with boatloads of divers and the bottom isn't covered with trash.

"Ok, well, if we are all in agreement, we need to collect some fees, sign the contracts and make some decisions." Jan showed Kate to their cabin while Tom and Hal brought their gear below.

"Dinner in an hour!" announced Jan. "As soon as the First Mate learns how to cook."

"Can I help with anything?" asked Kate. It was the first time she had offered to become a part of the crew.

"Well it's nothing fancy. We didn't know if you would be here today or tomorrow so we just planned on hamburgers and salad. So if you want to start the salad, the fridge is there. Make yourself at home."

"What can I do." Asked Tom.

"Can you run a charcoal barbecue?" Hal asked, reaching for the charcoal.

"Captain Hal, I believe I can handle that."

Hal decided to take the next step while still at the pier. He wanted to test their passengers. "Okay so what would you folks like for a pre-dinner drink? We have coffee, tea, sodas, water, beer, wine, rum and vodka."

Kate spoke up first, "Just a small white wine for me please."

Jan echoed her request. "That sounds good to me also."

Tom smiled, "So what are you having Captain?"

Hal reached into the cockpit fridge and retracted a beer. "It's a Pacifico for me, there is also some Corona.

"Corona sounds good to me. Thanks!" He stood to look after lighting the barbecue.

The Captain smiled and took a slug of beer. This might turn out to be all right. He thought. Yes sir, all right.

Morning dawned bright and clear with a slight northerly wind. In the cabin some confusion reigned as the new passengers found their way around. Hal suddenly found the boat a lot smaller. After breakfast they sat around the table in the galley studying a map.

"If we go east about twenty miles there is a good anchorage at Isla Tumafee. Then east of that there is a great spot called Lighthouse Reef. We can anchor above it and do some great diving and it the weather turns we can run back to Tumafee." He pointed these out on the map.

"Then depending on time and what you would like to do we could run up the coast about fifty miles to Punta Bonavista. There are some ruins there that make a nice dive, and a couple of wrecks on the outer banks."

Tom took a long pull at his beer. "Well Captain, Jesse said you knew your stuff, and Jesse saved my ass in 'Stan. He sure knows you. When you get us there we'll have a look. Hopefully we'll get some good pictures."

Jan put her hand on Hal's shoulder. "Kate is an underwater photographer, and Tom here is a writer. They are doing some research on Caribbean reef diving."

By noon Tumafee slid by their port side. The weather was perfect, the sea nearly calm, and the foursome were fast becoming friends. Hal still had reservations; nothing could go this smooth for long. He just sensed something unknown was imminent.

Chapter Twenty-Five

Hal watched for the water to change color to find the reef. Once over it he watched the depth finder until they had anchor depth under the keel.

"Okay Jan, let it go," he ordered.

The splash and rattle of chain confirmed the anchor had indeed been dropped. The two sailors busied themselves with lowering and stowing sails, securing halyards, and getting the boat ready for diving. Tom and Kate were making there own preparations. While Tom helped Hal with air tanks and regulators, Kate was busy with her camera. Tom wore a black suit while Kate had slipped into a light blue single piece outfit.

It became a little crowded in the cockpit with four people wearing tanks and large swim fins. As planned Jan was first to jump backwards off the boat. Kate went next, followed by Tom and lastly Hal splashed in. All four gave the thumbs up signal and Hal pointed downward. Four sparkling streams of bubbles followed the divers as they headed for the bottom. The depth at the top of the coral reef averaged about twenty-five feet. The actual bottom was a flat sand plateau at thirty-five feet. Toward the open sea the bottom dropped rapidly to several hundred feet, far beyond their capabilities. Tom scouted for photo opportunities while Kate snapped the camera. Hal and Jan hovered nearby, both enjoying the beauty of the reef, but monitoring their guests. The gentle motion of surface waves refracted the sun into moving beams of light traveling across the bottom. Hundreds of fish of every possible color swam among the polyps, sea fans, and sponges. The dark heads of moray eels protruded from several cave like openings. They were surrounded by a wonderland of color and motion.

Hal touched Jan's arm and pointed toward deeper water. The gliding gray shadow of a nurse shark startled her. It was the largest predator she had ever encountered. As it continued on its way he pointed out stingrays, octopus, and the now familiar groupers. She pointed excitedly at a large lobster, one of several they had found. Hal checked his dive watch and depth gauge. They had been down thirty minutes and it was time to ascend. He tapped his knife twice on the steel tank.

Tom and Kate, hearing the signal, turned to face the Dive Master.

Hal pointed upward. They swam to the anchor and slowly followed the line toward Sea Fever. Aboard the boat they laughed and giggled like school kids. It had been the first dive on a tropical reef for the Wakeman's. For Jan it had been her deepest to date and the first open ocean dive.

As they stripped off their gear Hal gave each piece a rinse in fresh water. The nearly empty air tanks were stored near the compressor and fresh ones brought out.

"So, how was it?" Asked the new Captain.

The first reply came from Kate. "Fantastic! Just absolutely fantastic! I can't wait to see the photos.

"It is a dream come true." Said Tom. "We have waited for years to do this trip."

"So can we spend a few days on this reef, or do you want to go somewhere else?" asked Hal.

"This good for me." Kate volunteered. "It can't get much better. Can it?"

Jan finished toweling her hair before asking. "Are

we finished diving for the day? If so I think a celebratory cocktail is in order."

"Suits me." Voted Tom. "I am a little beat after that." Kate nodded her head in agreement.

Hal stood and put on the artificial foot. "Then I think we'll run back to the island. We're not going to stay out here all night."

As if they had been together for years all hands set to and quickly weighed the anchor, hoisted the sails, and got under way Jan soon appeared from the galley with a tray of frosted glasses and a pitcher of greenish liquid.

"I sure hope everyone likes margaritas." She poured the drinks and handed them around.

The early afternoon breeze gathered strength and Sea Fever was soon racing along. White foam formed at her bow and a long wake behind marked her passing.

Hal looked at the sky. "It looks like we may get a squall tonight. I think we'll anchor on the north side of the island."

By late afternoon they were entering a quiet cove, away from the rising winds. Jan was in the galley starting dinner so Tom and Kate pitched in to help Hal.

"Does anyone live on this island?" asked Kate.

Hal shook his head. "From what I've been told there is no fresh water on the island. It is mainly a picnic, diving, and fishing spot. So no one lives here."

Kate stared shoreward as she continued. "Might we go ashore and explore it?"

"Sure the dinghy will hold the four of us. We could pack a lunch and make a day of it." Hal liked the idea immediately. "How about we go early in the morning before it gets too warm?"

After dinner they were relaxing on deck. The feeble yellow light from a kerosene-fueled hurricane lamp was barely bright enough to throw shadows.

"So Tom," Hal began. "What do you do for a living?"

Tom glanced nervously at Kate. She shook her head in a barely perceptible motion. Jan saw the reaction and immediately suspected their guests were hiding something. "Well lets just say I was in the military," he finally replied Hal put his stump across his opposite knee and began rubbing the scar.

"Really? So were Jan and I, in fact that's how we first met. She was a combat nurse and a Taliban RPG chopped me up. That's where I left this foot and fingers. I was a diver, underwater demolition and obstruction clearance."

Tom seemed to loosen up. "Well there's a coincidence for you." His wife nodded her head "I was a Navy Seal, that's where I got my dive training. Kate here was a combat helicopter pilot aboard the ship I was on. Her machine took some anti-aircraft fire over Kuwait. My team and I went in and brought her and the crew out. We kept in touch and married when we left the navy."

The evening passed quickly as they told jokes and war stories. Their nearly continuous laughter rolled across the bay, heard by no one else.

The first light of the rising sun found the foursome enjoying breakfast in the galley. As they finished the last of the coffee Hal went up on deck.

The girls soon had the dishes cleared away and prepared to go ashore. Tom slipped into a pair of shorts and joined Hal topside. With Tom's help they soon had the smaller boat in the water. Hal checked the fuel, put in the oars and four life jackets. The girls busied themselves with a lunch and Kate gathered her camera gear. By the time the sun had risen above the island they were ready.

Hal held the dinghy steady while the others

boarded then followed them. He soon had the tiny outboard motor purring and it carried them toward the beach. Below them was another shallow reef. It teemed with marine life and the water was beginning to show the ultramarine color in the sunlight. They beached the boat and ran a line to a nearby palm tree. Sand crabs scattered in all directions as they approached. They walked among the palms and soon found an old trail leading into the jungle. Machete in hand Hal led the way, chopping the newest growth from their path. Since the island had no water it did not support any animal life. But the birds made up for it. There were hundreds of species, of every imaginable color, flitting through the trees.

Kate's camera was kept busy trying to capture the images.It took nearly an hour to cross the island. They emerged from the jungle on a white beach identical to the one they had arrived on.

Hot and sweaty from the trail work Hal kept walking forward and dove into the sea. Soon, as if on signal, the four of them were cavorting in the crystal clear water.

"Anyone hungry?" Called Jan. Kate helped her spread the blanket in a shady spot under the palms. They each picked their choice from the stacks of sandwiches. Jan had made egg salad, ham and cheese, and corned beef on rye. Hal was handing out cold cans of beer. As they finished lunch they discussed plans for the rest of the day. Tom popped the last of his sandwich into his mouth. After washing it down with a slug of beer he made a suggestion.

"Why don't we walk the beach around the island? There is more to see than there is plowing through the jungle.

"Good idea honey." Agreed Kate. "I have enough pictures of trees."

Four sets of footprints in the sand soon became the only trace of their visit. Late afternoon found four tired hikers resting aboard Sea Fever. The walk around the island had been farther than they had figured on.

Hal motioned to Tom to join him in the after section of the cockpit.

"I don't expect any trouble," he began. "But just to let you know we are prepared." He let the sentence hang as he raised the lid of the bench.

"Mm yeah, I'd say you are prepared." Tom recognized the familiar shape. "It's a bit different than the M-16's we had.

"It's a Canadian C-7 but almost the same."

Tom lifted the launcher. "And grenades?" he asked.

Hal pointed to a green box, "Three high explosive and six phosphorous smoke."

Tom chuckled, "Well now I feel better." He reached into the cabin for his backpack. From it he pulled a package wrapped in plastic. Unwrapping it partially he showed it to Hal.

The Captain whistled quietly, "An Ingram? And probably nine millimeter?"

"Yep, and Kate has her Glock automatic, also nine millimeter and between us we have fifty rounds of soft points. Just in case!"

"Wow, it's a good thing Mexican customs didn't find them. That is an automatic thirty years hard time in a Mexican prison."

Tom re-wrapped the little black machine gun. "Yes, well, lets just say that they were waiting for us when we arrived. There has been too much killing going on down here since the doper gangs and cartels started their little turf wars. I'll be damned if I am going to stay home, as long as I have some firepower."

"Well with any luck, we won't need them."

Chapter Twenty-Six

The next morning the group decided to dive the reef in this protected bay. Hal had seen some dark shadows along the reef so he added a Bang-Stick to his regular gear.

"What is that thing?" asked Jan Hal unscrewed the end of the aluminum tube and inserted a shotgun shell from his belt.

"I think I saw a few sharks this morning. This is just in case one of them decides to get hungry. It will kill just about anything in these waters. "

"What kind of sharks?" Asked Kate.

"Oh it's hard to say, there are about thirty different species and many of them travel a lot so you never know. The odds of getting attacked are worse than winning a lottery but you never know. This is just in case."

He proceeded to remove a couple of spear guns from the dive locker. "Now these guys are for shopping. We could use some lobster or a couple of nice fish for supper."

Tom and Kate took the guns and went over the side. Soon they were prowling the edge of the reef. Jan and Hal hovered over them, relaxing and just enjoying the swim. Kate giggled in her mouthpiece; several small blue and yellow fish were up close to her face-mask, looking into her eyes. She regretted not bringing a camera; this would have made a great photo. . A distinct metallic click signaled someone cocking a spear gun. A moment later the sliding squeak of metal on metal announced a shot. Tom appeared holding a spear with a large lobster securely impaled on his spear. His face radiant with success. Hal helped him remove his catch and reload the spear. Tom had just returned to the reef when they heard Kate's weapon fire. She, too, produced a nice sized lobster.

Before their tanks ran low on air they had four crustaceans in Hal's dive bag and a nice trout still on Tom's spear. Hal gave the signal to surface. A trail of blood streamed behind them as they rose to the surface.

From behind the reef came a large shark. Sensing the blood from the trout it made the natural decision to have an easy meal. Kate saw a movement in the corner of her eye and turned for a better look. She screamed into her mouthpiece as she saw the gaping mouth full of teeth coming from behind her husband. Hearing the scream, Hal spun around. The shark circled, as if measuring the risk. He snapped off the safety on the bang stick and swam toward the endangered diver. A movement of the spear caused another jet of blood from the fish.

Tom was still unaware of the shark. It came straight at him, the hideous mouth gaping. Hal knew that if the shark grabbed the fish he might take Tom's arm with it. Finally realizing what Hal was doing, Tom looked to his rear. The shark was getting close, on a direct course for the trout. He had no time to react. Hal had the shark killer at arms-length when it met the side of the beast's head. There came a muffled bang and a red cloud of blood-tinged water, accompanied by a smoke filled bubble. The would- be man-eater rolled over and slowly drifted downward blood pouring from the gaping hole in its head. The smoky bubble rose upward, bursting silently at the surface. The foursome boarded the yacht in silence.

Tom was still pale from the near miss.

"I hated to kill it," said Hal quietly. But I don't think it would have stopped with that little trout. Once they smell blood they usually go into a feeding frenzy.

"If only I had dropped the damned trout," muttered Tom. "Hey buddy, it wouldn't have helped. The spear is on a lanyard back to the gun and you. Besides, it had scented blood; it doesn't matter if it was yours or the fish. He was going to attack anyway."

Kate joined in, "Won't the dead one's blood attract more?

"You bet it will. So we won't be diving here again right away."Hal reloaded the Bang Stick and returned it to the dive locker.

After descending the companionway steps, Jan busied herself in the galley. She soon emerged on deck carrying a tray. "After that we need to splice something, I have Margaritas for everyone."

They had toasted each other for a good day and Kate went below. After a period of clattering and banging from the galley she reappeared.

"Cacahuates anyone?" She started a tray of munchies around the cockpit. Tom eyeballed the tray,

"Cock a whaties?" He asked.

"Cacahuates," repeated his wife. "But for you gringos, they're peanuts."

Hal put a bucket out to throw shells in, but the deck was soon littered with the near misses. The Captain stood and hoisted the bag of seafood.

"Tom if you'll give me a hand we'll get these lobsters and your trout cleaned up and on the grill. The girls can whip up a salad or something."

Working together the two men soon had their catch ready. Hal tossed the guts over the side and rinsed off his hands. "I don't know about you my friend, but to me a beer would be better than another margarita."

Tom nodded in agreement and Hal retrieved two cans from the cooler. He then passed the pitcher of lime, lemon and tequila to the girls in the galley. "That should cause some giggling before long."

"Honey," called Hal. "Would you pass me that butter basting sauce from the fridge please?"

Jan handed him a bowl with a basting brush in it. He applied a liberal coating to the lobsters and the fish.

"I'll let that marinate a few minutes while the grill heats." He lit the grill and rejoined Tom, opening another beer.

They were just beginning their dinner when a large speedboat roared across the opening of the bay.

"Wow!" Said Tom. "That's a fast boat."

"It sure is," commented Hal. "It looks like one of those Cigarette type ocean racers. It must be going seventy miles per hour. The first boat was nearly out of sight when another appeared. Above the roar of engines they could hear a booming sound.

"That's a Coast Guard Cutter." Said Tom, standing to get a better look. "And they are firing the deck gun at that speedboat.

"Right." Hal grabbed his binoculars to get a better look. Within seconds both vessels were out of sight. "They must be running dope, or else they're pirates."

The sound of engines soon faded. The heavy gunfire had ceased. Jan looked at Hal. "Do you think they caught them?"

"It's hard to say, there are dozens of small islands just west of here. If he knows his way around he might get away." The foursome resumed their dinner.

"Hal this lobster is first rate," offered Tom. "Nice job."

The ladies also offered compliments to the Captain.

Jan giggled, "So that makes you our Captain

Cook."

Everyone laughed at her humor. Hal held up his injured hand. "Yes well I almost became Captain Hook."

Tom could not refuse the opening, pointing at Hal's stump. "I don't know about that, but you could pass as Pegleg the Pirate."

Jan frowned at Tom, "That will be Captain Pegleg to you!"

Kate surprised them all when she jumped in. "Careful Guys! He just might decide to make you walk the plank."

The sun was long gone and the only light was from a small bulb in the galley. Overhead the night sky glistened with millions of stars. The gentle rocking of the boat in the lee of the island had caused them all to relax. The drama of the shark had passed.

"Well this has been an interesting day," offered Hal. "What do you suppose tomorrow will bring? And speaking of tomorrow, we have four more days. What would you guys like to do?"

Kate quickly answered. "Is there anywhere nearby that we can dive to some Mayan Ruins? I'd love to get some pictures of an underwater temple."

Hal scratched his head. "There are some sunken ruins near Tulum. It would take nearly a day to reach it, and I have never dived there. It's open water so we might be in for some rough seas, but we could try it."

Tom agreed, "Okay as long as there are no hungry sharks, dope running speedboats. Or Pegleg pirates."

Hal had been thinking about the Coast Guard's running gun battle. If this island was on a smuggling route it might be wise to leave before another outlaw boat passed by. He had the old feeling back again, like when the shrimpers had returned.

Chapter Twenty-Seven

As usual the first rays of morning sunlight found Hal on deck with a cup of coffee. From the weather radio came details of the forecast for the following week. He listened intently; the information would affect his decision for their destination. The broadcast ended just as Jan emerged from the galley.

"Good forecast?" She asked as she tipped her head upward for a good morning kiss.

"It sounds okay, nothing serious coming in." Together they sat on the bench near the helm, enjoying the arrival of a new day. Jan rose to fill their cups just as Kate's head appeared.

"You two lovebirds want more coffee?" She teased. "I'm coming up anyway."

When they heard Tom get up and move around they went below. Breakfast was a simple meal of toast, fresh fruit, cottage cheese, and coffee. They had just finished eating when Kate raised her hand and said. "Listen."

Then they all heard it. The distant but approaching sound of a boat engine grew slowly louder

"It doesn't sound right." Said Tom. "Like it's missing or knocking or something."

Hal went up on deck and took out his binoculars. He was scanning through the palms on the spit, looking at the sea beyond.

"Aww Shit!"

The others heard his expletive in the galley. Tom

ran up the stairs to join the

Captain.

"What is it?" he asked.

"It looks like the boat that the Coast Guard was chasing yesterday. It's moving slow and trailing smoke. It will be at the entrance to the bay in a minute or two."

Tom stroked his unshaven chin, "Do you think they will bother us?"

"If they're dope runners in a shot up boat they'll be looking for a new ride. We just might fit their plans. Except I think we'll have a surprise waiting for them." Hal stored the glasses and opened the bench locker. The C7 rifle and launcher were soon loaded and ready.

Tom went below and unpacked his miniature machine gun and his wife's pistol.

"Tom you go forward to the vee-birth and open the deck hatch. I'll stay here and the girls can stay below. If things get nasty we can get them in a crossfire. But we need them to get close, that Ingram doesn't have the range of the C7."

Hal watch the smoking boat, hoping it would continue past the island. It didn't.

There were three men in the cockpit of the sleek race boat as it approached Sea Fever. They were less than one hundred yards away when a voice came across the water.

"Hello the sail boat." Said a man's voice in English. There was no Mexican accent.

In the cabin Jan's face suddenly paled. She climbed the companionway and stuck her head out for a better look. The other boats engine stopped. Only one of the big V-8s had been running.

"We seem to have a problem here, could you help us out?" The smoking boat was drifting closer. Hal could see a row of bullet holes along the port side.

They had escaped the Coast Guard but not before getting shot up.

"Again the voice from the approaching boat. "We need a ride to Belize City. I would be glad to pay you." From behind his back he heard a choking whisper from Jan.

"Dick?" Was all she could say.

"Carol, you rotten bitch" Said the man at the helm on the other boat. Sea Fever's Captain raised the C7 to the ready position, it could now be seen by the other crew. The forward hatch on the drifting boat suddenly flew open. A fourth man appeared. He held an AK-47 assault rifle and was swinging it toward the big yacht. Tom didn't hesitate. From his hidden spot in the sailboat's bow he fired a long burst.

The little nine millimeter sub-machine gun roared as a dozen shells cycled through the action. The AK-47 splashed into the sea as the man sprawled across the deck

In the cockpit two more guns appeared, a rifle and a pistol. Hal had his weapon already set for burst. The pistol barked as its owner tried a fast shot, it missed and he fired again. The second round also went wide, and it was his last.

Three red blotches appeared on his chest as Hal triggered the C7. The rifleman was swinging his barrel toward Hal while his fellow crewman lifted the small machine gun. The roar of the C7, now on full automatic, joined the rapid-fire sound from the bow. Both battle-seasoned veterans took their targets with deadly effect.

"You Okay Tom?' Shouted Hal.

"Roger that." Came the response from the bow. "I'm just watching for any movement over there." Glancing below Hal checked the cabin. Kate held her Glock at the ready but both women were fine. The incoming tide brought the other boat closer. As it neared, Hal stepped aboard, his rifle still ready. A quick check of the four bodies confirmed they were all dead. He released the boats anchor then returned to Sea Fever.

When Hal dropped to the galley he found Kate comforting Jan. The latter was pale and shaking. The look in her eyes reflected cold hard fear.

"Jan honey, what's wrong? She looked up, her lips trembling. "That was Dick!" She blurted. Hal was dumbstruck for a moment.

"Dick? Your dead husband? You said he was killed in Afghanistan. What the hell are you talking about?"

Jan was crying now. Kate was still holding her and Tom had joined the group.

"It was all a lie Hal. I'm so sorry." She sobbed.

"What was a lie? What happened?"

Jan wiped her eyes and looked up at Hal. "My real name is Carol Davis. Dick Davis, my ex-husband, was dealing drugs in Montreal. Six years ago he got caught and sentenced to ten years in prison. While he was in there I divorced him, changed my name, and joined the army. He swore he would find me and kill me for deserting him. Four months ago I heard he got an early parole. I knew he would be looking for me so I ran to Mexico. You know the rest of the story."

Hal shook his head; it took a few minutes to absorb what she had said. "Did you know he was running a boat down here?

"No Hal, I didn't. I thought he would go back to his old buddies in Montreal. The army knew about what had happened. When I told them he was loose they offered to send me overseas, anywhere I wanted to go. When I said no I just wanted out, they released me."

Tom busied himself at the galley bar. He soon had a double rum Cuba Libre ready for each of them.

"Hey folks, time to splice that thing again."

Hal accepted the drink and sat down. "Tom, Kate, you didn't hire us for this kind of trip. I'll refund your money and take you ashore wherever you want to go."

Kate shook her head. Before she could speak Tom roared back his answer "Like hell you will." You still owe me three days cruising and reef diving. Besides my friend, I came ready for trouble. I am just glad you did too. We make one hell of a fire team."

Hal reached for the radiotelephone. Moments later he was connected to the Captain of the cutter that had chased this boat earlier. They were less than thirty miles away and arrived in the bay in under an hour. By the time the Coast Guard arrived the speedboat was nearly full of water. They put two crewmen aboard with a pump and began to remove the water. The four drug dealers were put in body bags and transferred to the cutter.

A brief report was written up, signed by the four divers, and the cutter departed towing the bullet-riddled hulk behind. The foursome finished their drinks and Tom mixed four more. The mood was somber. Each felt lucky that they had won the gunfight, but killing is never a pleasant task. Jan was still morose. Her life, her future, and her happiness depended on Hal.

"Hal honey, what does this mean for us? I know I lied but I had to." She burst into tears again. "That bastard screwed up my life once, and now he has done it again. Do you hate me for that?"

Hal sat beside her and took her in his arms. "Sweetheart, none of this was your fault. You did what you had to do. Besides, if you hadn't been running from him we would never have met. It's over, let's just put the pieces back together and pick it up where we left off." He lifted her chin and kissed her. The saltiness of her tears wet his lips He now realized that Jan'sex-husband comment that he had silently questioned hadn't been an innocent slip of the tongue after all. They would have to work out whether she would remain Janice or change back to Carol.

Tom spoke up and broke the tension. "Okay you two, suck it up! We have a cruise ship to run and that reef is just sittin' there waiting for us."

Working together the foursome raised the sails and soon left the place they would now call 'Bad Luck Bay. Hal set a course for Tulum. They might have to sail all night to get there but leaving that bay was important. Hal still had a bad feeling. Somehow he knew this was not yet over. He had doubled his normal attentiveness. Somewhere, someone was still seeking him. It was a feeling that he was in a sniper's sights. Just waiting for a bullet.

Chapter Twenty-Eight

They cruised all day under sail, making good time despite light winds. Hal had entered the coordinates for Punta Herrero in the GPS.

The instrument now indicated they were less than four miles from their next course change. They rounded the point into Bahia del Espiritu Santo just as the sun was setting. Hal sailed a mile into the bay before deciding they had enough protection from the open sea.

"Ok, Jan drop the main and the jib. Tom you can drop the hook here." As the sails came down and the anchor splashed Hal was searching the beach with the powerful binoculars. The feeling he was being watched or hunted sent shivers down his back. Tom had secured the anchor line and came aft to the cockpit.

"What's up Hal? You look spooked.'

"Just a hunch. All day I've felt like someone was watching me or looking for me."

"Hey Cap. Relax a bit, with all the shooting and crap around you two it's no wonder you are getting jumpy. Jan told us about the way you met. You guys have a habit of running into some real bad dudes. But hey man, I've got your back, and the girls have got mine. So chill out."

Jan and Kate finished securing the sails then went below. In just a few moments they were back on deck carrying trays.

"Now how the hell did you get that stuff ready so fast?" Asked Hal.

"Oh you silly man, we had this ready an hour ago. We were wondering if you were ever going to stop."

Hal took a beer from one tray and a handful of nachos from the other. "I'll be back. He warned, looking over the assorted snacks before sitting down.

In the growing darkness they drank beer and feasted on nachos and salsa. The second tray also held sliced cheese, pickles, olives, smoked oysters, and a ring of precooked shrimp and sauce. The evening passed quickly with small talk, stories, and an occasional joke. Sea Fever swung gently in the dying breeze, her anchor holding firmly on the coral reef beneath her.

Hal and Jan sat on the port bench, their arms encircling each other. Tom and Kate were similarly seated on the opposite side. A long period of silence ended as Kate spoke," Hey Jan, do you guys ever go skinny dipping?"

Jan was glad of the darkness as she felt a blush creep across her face. "Um, yeah, we have actually. Why?"

"Well Tom and I really enjoy it and we would like to dive nude with the SCUBA gear. Would you guys mind?"

Jan looked to Hal for an answer, his face barely visible in the darkness. The Captain just shrugged his shoulders, this was girl talk and he wasn't committing himself. "I don't see any problem, we might even join you. But don't even think about any funny stuff. We do not swap, share, or do group sex. Just so we all know the rules."

She put her hand on Hal's bare knee and squeezed. She had also missed the privacy that allowed them to swim nude together. Except now there would be no sexual encounters on the seabed.

They got an early start just after dawn and by mid-morning the anchor splashed near Tulum. Hal wasn't exactly sure where the undersea ruins were, and discussed it with Tom.

"It would make sense if they were right opposite the ruins on top of the cliff." Suggested the second diver.

Hal held a map and checked the Fathometer. "We're right over a structure of some kind, either a wall or a reef. But wherever it is the ruins can't be that far away. Lets get into the gear and put in a dive before lunch."

Tom ran the diving flag up the port halyard while Hal prepared their gear. The square red pennant with a white diagonal stripe would tell others that there were divers down. The girls appeared on deck wearing swimsuits.

"No skinny-dipping?" Teased Hal

Jan pointed to the top of the nearby cliff. The main pyramid of the old Mayan temple was crawling with tourists. "Not in public, thank you."

"Sea Fever, Sea Fever, Sea Fever, This is Mexican coast guard Chetumal Calling sailing vessel Sea Fever, over."

Hal jumped to his feet and grabbed the microphone on the marine radio.

"Mexican Coast Guard Chetumal this is Sea Fever, Over."

"Sea Fever this is Chetumal; I have a request for you over.

"Chetumal go ahead, over.

"Sea Fever, The Comandante, Coast Guard Chetumal, sends his regards and requests you meet him at Chetumal or at Playa del Carman within the next few days. Over.

"Chetumal, my position now is near Tulum, I say

again Tulum. I can be in Playa late tomorrow. Over.

"Sea Fever I copy Playa late tomorrow. Thank you, Chetumal Out."

Hal replaced the microphone. "Now what the hell do you suppose that was all about?"

Tom laughed, "Well one thing for damned sure. If they were going to arrest you they sure as hell wouldn't ask you to meet the Comandante."

"No I guess not, but that cuts our diving here to this afternoon. Sorry about that guys."

Soon four trails of rising bubbles again followed their descent. Hal had been pretty close to the underwater portion of Tulum. Even at a depth of thirty feet the water seemed crystal clear. A thousand years of wind, waves, storms and tides had taken their toll on the ancient buildings.

Out in front Kate cavorted through the ruins. Like a big fish she swam in though a window and out through a door. The nooks and crannies between the stone blocks were home to thousands of colorful reef dwellers. She hung motionless above the others, signaling them to follow her path. Her ready camera recorded the scene and the surrounding buildings.

They circled and explored for nearly forty minutes when Hal signaled it was time to surface. Following the rules of safe diving they drifted slowly upward. The danger of damaged lungs from the compressed air was reduced by never ascending faster than the bubbles.

The foursome surfaced near the boat and Kate hung back as the others boarded. Her camera recorded the view of the divers and the boat with the ruins of Tulum at the top of the cliff behind them.

* * * *

Early the next morning they were underway again,

heading for the Coast Guard Base at Playa Del Carman.

"I sure hope this is nothing serious." Said Jan, a worried note in her voice.

Hal shook his head, "Probably just more paperwork about those guys in the speedboat."

"Just as long as we don't end up in a Mexican prison." Added Kate, "I hear they're terrible places."

Hal shook his head again. "Whatever this is about, you guys are not involved. You are paying customers on this cruise and I am responsible for all activities aboard this vessel. I am thinking of letting you off first, then Jan and I will see what this is all about."

"Like hell you will." Shouted Tom. "If this is about those dopers, I was shooting too. If you hadn't had that C7 and opened up with it we would probably all be fish food by now. Customers my ass! If you go down we all go down."

"Well we'll know before long, there is the entrance to the harbor Let's get the sails down and we'll motor in. I see a dock with a Coast Guard boat tied up." Hal started the diesel while the others went to work.

As they pulled alongside the dock two uniformed men appeared and asked for the mooring lines. As soon as Sea Fever was made fast to the dock one of the men spoke.

"Capitan Sigurdson welcome to Playa Del Carman. My Comandante is waiting for you in his office. If you wish your wife and your friends may also come along."

Hal was baffled. If he was in trouble they were being very nice about it. It must be just more paperwork, he thought.

The four sailors were soon following the uniformed guardsman toward a modern brick building. A series of flags billowed from several masts in the courtyard. Their escort led them directly to the office of the Commander.

As they entered he rose from his desk and saluted them. His full dress uniform made an impression with numerous medals and gold braid. "Please sit down." He invited. Then he removed his cap and returned to his seat. "I have no doubt my friends that you are wondering about the urgency and the reason why I asked you to come here."

The officer's English was nearly perfect with only a trace of his Hispanic mother tongue. "I wanted to be sure to meet you before you sailed back to Estado Unitos. Excuse me, the United States. My government appreciates very much your assistance in ending the careers of several people involved in the drug trade. In particular we on this station thank you, one of our members lost his life while our cutter attempted to stop that speedboat." He retrieved an envelope from a desk drawer, a large smile on his face.

"My friends, you probably did not know it but there was a very large reward for the capture of each of those drug runners. The state of Quintaneroo and the Mexican government have asked me to present this to you."

He pushed a type written form across the desk to a bewildered sailing Captain.

"If you will sign this receipt I will give you a check to cash at your convenience or to deposit at your leisure. As Captain it is your choice if you wish to share this with your crew."

Hal took the pen offered to him and scanned the paper. The names of each of the men they had killed were listed opposite the amount of the rewards posted. The bottom of the page revealed the total amount. The figure was staggering, P 1,000,000.

It took but a second for the Dive Master to do a quick calculation to convert the amount from Pesos to Dollars. Hal looked at Jan, Tom and Kate. Each had quizzical expressions, wondering what the amount was. He signed the paper and a duplicate.

The Comandante rose offered his hand to Hal and with the other hand handed over a brown envelope. "And now Captain, the Sea Fever is free to go, and you sail with the thanks of the Mexican people."

Hal tried to remain serious as he walked from the building. It was not until they were aboard the boat that he released his pent-up emotions. He kissed Jan long and hard, then hugged and kissed Kate and put his arms around Tom. He put the receipt on the table for everyone to see.

"A million Pesos! That is almost a hundred thousand dollars."

Jan's chin dropped. Tom and Kate were also open mouthed. This was far beyond the wildest expectations of any of them. Jan was the first to recover.

"Hal remember that white wine we had after we met, the stuff I can't pronounce?"

"You mean that Gewurtstraminer?"

"Yes, I have been saving a bottle for a special occasion. This is as special as it gets." She took the bottle out of the fridge. Next she put four glasses on the table. She handed Hal the bottle. "If you would do the honors sir?"

Hal soon had the cork out of the frosty brown bottle. He filled the glasses with the light amber colored liquid. As each took a glass he proposed a toast. "To the best damned crew that ever hoisted sail and strapped on a tank." As he sat down he began to wonder how he would divide the reward, and what he would do with his share.

Chapter Twenty-Nine

Playa del Carman did not have a bank with connections to his home bank so Hal decided to sail to Cancun to cash the check. All the way there he tried to think of the best way to spit the reward, if in fact he did decide to share. After all it was his boat. He was the Captain. Or he could split it four ways, but that wouldn't be fair to Jan. That way Tom and Kate would get half of the money and Jan would get a quarter. If he and Tom split the pot Kate would still get half, with Tom, but Jan would get nothing. He had a headache from just thinking about it.

They were riding a freshening breeze from the southwest. The boat was making good time and the sea was fairly calm. Tom and Kate had moved up to the bow where they sat talking in the shade of the jib sail. The wind carried their voices away so Hal could hear nothing.

In the galley Jan kept herself busy by preparing lunch. Hal had mixed feelings about this being the last day of the cruise. He had enjoyed the company of the other couple but they suffered from a lack of privacy. It had been just two weeks since they had last enjoyed sex together, but it seemed like months. If they were going to continue this cruise business maybe they should find a bigger boat. He began running the figures through his head. With what they could get for this boat, plus their share of the reward, maybe they could buy a bigger vessel.

Jan came topside and put her arm around Hal's

waist. She looked up at him and smiled.

"What?" He asked. Jan leaned her head against his shoulder. "There will be only the two of us on board tonight." She whispered softly.

"Um, yeah, that's what I was just thinking."

She glanced forward. The others were looking ahead. Her hand slipped down Hal's chest, and stopped on the prominent bulge in his slacks. She gave it a tender little squeeze then kissed his bare shoulder and disappeared below.

For the second time since buying this boat his mind jumped to a different track. A sudden thought became prominent. Was he ready yet? Did he want to get married again? He wondered if Jan was ready. He worshiped the girl. She was smart, good looking, responsible, and he wanted to be near her. There was no doubt that they enjoyed fantastic sex. But was he in love with her?

Jan sat in the cabin almost in a daze. Whether through mental telepathy or pure coincidence the same thoughts had been running through her mind. There was a difference; she knew she was madly in love with this wild and wonderful man. She was beginning to feel like a wife should feel. She was wanted, protected, included in his activities, and addicted to his lovemaking skills.

As they approached the Cancun harbor entrance Tom and Kate came aft to the cockpit. Tom leaned on the compass binnacle and cleared his throat.

"Um Skipper," he began. "We need to talk."

Hal eased the helm and swung a bit to starboard, slowing the boat. "Okay," he said. "But can we get the sails down and get tied up first?"

Jan heard the exchange and joined the others on deck. Hal turned Sea Fever into the wind and they worked together to lower and reef the sails. While the others finished securing the halyards the Captain started the diesel.

Hal was maneuvering through the dozens of boats anchored in the harbor and at the marina. Tom got the bow mooring line ready while Kate looked after the stern. Jan busied herself getting the inflatable rubber bumpers over the side. As they approached a vacant slip Hal spun the wheel to port, shifted the engine to reverse, and opened the throttle.

As the boat stopped He shut off the engine, Tom and Kate jumped to the slip and Jan gave him a thumbs up.

"Nice job honey." She added.

With the boat secured Hal gave Jan a slap on the butt. "Nice job yourself, now for those of you that haven't noticed, it is beer-thirty."

Jan took the hint and went below. In a moment she returned with four cans of beer. "These are the last we have."

The Other couple returned aboard as Hal sat on the cockpit bench. "Now what's up with you guys?"

Tom looked over at Kate. She nodded and he took a mouthful of beer "Well, it's this way. We have been talking about that reward."

Hal jumped in, "Yes, well." is as far as he got.

"Just listen for a minute," Tom was trying to keep his voice down. "First of all you haven't said a word about that money. We don't know if you are going to keep it or split it or what. But Kate and I had an idea that we want to ask you about." He took another swig of beer. "We may be way out to lunch here but what the hell. We all get along, we know what we're doing, and we have a chance to do something together. Kate and I wondered if you guys would consider a partnership, or at least taking us on as crew. We could run one hell of a cruise business. Maybe we could even get a bigger boat. So what do you think?"

Jan looked at Hal, she was wide eyed with surprise. Hal sipped some more beer. "Well, first things first. I hadn't decided how we would split the reward. So we would have to discuss that. As far as a business or a bigger boat, I had been thinking along the same lines. If we took all the rewardmoney and sank it into a business we could form a partnership with all four as equal partners."

He turned to his lady friend. "Jan, you're a part of this, which way would you rather go. Split the cash, form a company, buy a boat or maybe you have another idea?'

Jan sat down beside Hal. "Honey, we've been together on this boat for two weeks without a bad word among us. I would vote for a company but yes a bigger boat. There is just not much privacy on this one."

Hal smiled and raised his beer in a salute. "So I guess this is the first board meeting of the company and I move we named it 'Reef Dive Veteran Cruise Company. '

"I second the motion," Jan clapped her hands as she spoke. "All in favor?" Asked Hal. Everyone raised his or her hands. "Carried!"

"So the next order of business is to discuss the reward. Then a newer, or bigger boat." Continued the Captain.

Tom spoke up. "First of all, as Captain I think you should be the president. If that is acceptable to all, I think the reward money should go straight into the company and be earmarked for another boat and more diving gear."

As the afternoon passed they discussed further details of the new company. Then Tom went up to the marina office to buy a U. S. newspaper and a Used Yacht Magazine. Back on board the girls were preparing dinner while the guys perused the ads for a boat they could use. The discussion that followed pertained to the type of boat. Would they stay with a motor sailer? Or go with a straight power cruiser?

That night Hal came to another decision. It was time to get on with his life. While the others slept he was busy with a long narrow piece of sailcloth, black paint, and needle and thread.

In the morning Jan went on deck as usual to enjoy her morning coffee. Hearing the rattle of a loose halyard she turned to face the mast. Unknown to her Hal was waiting in the companionway. Looking up she was astonished. From the top of the mast was a long vertical sign. In large black letters it read;

JAN MARRY ME?

She turned to face the cabin and saw Hal. He was down on one knee and in his hand he held a rough ring he had fashioned from a brass washer. "Please?" was all he said.

It was enough, Jan offered her left hand and he slipped the ring on. Then she spoke, one word but that was all he wanted to hear. "Yes!"

He stood and took her in his arms. The kiss was long, hot and deep. She was breathless when they finally parted.

Tom and Kate came on deck. They noticed the sign and Tom remarked, "So that's what you were up doing last night?"

Kate went to Jan and hugged her. Both girls had tears in their eyes as the congratulations flowed.

Hal looked Jan in the eye, "But we have some other problems." He said.

Jan looked at him, wondering what he would come up with next. "Well we have to go shopping for a ring, then we have to decide where and when we get married. Then there is the wedding plans, invitations, reception, and where will we honeymoon?"

Jan smiled, and again a tear showed in her eye. "Okay on the ring, but do we need a big elaborate wedding? We have no family, why not keep it simple? As far as a honeymoon, well if we have this boat or a company boat?"

She stopped in mid-sentence as Hal grasped her hand. He looked into her eyes as he spoke. "Um, there is one other little problem we need to iron out. I don't know if we could legally get married with your name as Northwaite. So how do we get around that?"

Jan smiled back at him and shook her head. "The army said I couldn't sign up with a fake name so they helped me get it legally changed. Carol Davis is buried in my past, and she will stay there. So if you think that's an excuse not to get married you can forget it."

Hal took her in his arms again and whispered in her ear. "Okay, well that's a good thing. I don't think I could get used to you suddenly being a Carol. As far as the honeymoon goes we could have a sneak preview right now."

"I heard that," laughed Tom, I think Kate and I have some shopping to do, we should be back tomorrow. You can take that sign down when you are ready to leave, or when you want us to come back."

Chapter Thirty

Their new business partners had no sooner left the boat than the betrothed couple disappeared below decks. Tom and Kate looked back and smiled, knowing what was happening in the master cabin.

Hal took Jan in his arms and what started out as a gentle kiss soon became a madly passionate embrace.

"Mmmm two months is a long time," he said, his hands sliding to her breasts.

"It hasn't been two months and you know it. It hasn't even been two weeks." She lifted his T-shirt over his head.

"Well it's been a very long two weeks." He unsnapped her bra and it joined her shirt on the floor.

Jan fumbled with his belt but he pushed her backwards onto the bed before she got it undone. He took her shoes off then slid her slacks down and added them to the growing pile.

Now clad in just her panties she rolled him over and attacked his belt buckle. As soon as it was undone she pulled the snap apart and slid the zipper down. He arched his back so she could get his pants off. He rolled back on top and kissed her, their tongues searching and tasting. His hand stroked her cheek. Then slid slowly down to cup and caress her breast. Her nipples hardened at his touch.

She reached down and slid her hand into his briefs. Knowing what would be there she still felt a shivering thrill of anticipation as his hardness filled her hand. It felt somehow different, knowing now it was more than sex between them. She loved this man more than she had ever loved anyone. She wanted him for love, but also for the wild and wonderful coupling they were about to enjoy.

He slid down and took a nipple in his mouth, savoring it. First one, and then the other, he licked and sucked each in turn. Slowly, teasingly his hand slid down across her tummy. The silken panties, wet with her juices, moistened his fingers as he slid his hand over them and covered her mound. Lifting the elastic at her waist he slipped into the full growth of hair covering her entrance. His fingers found the cleft and touched the protruding nub of her clitoris.

His touch at her opening brought another electric shiver. She pushed at his briefs, struggling to remove them. He in turn was removing her final covering. Hal slid downward, kissing his way lower. Her scent was a wonderful welcome, as his tongue tasted her. He spread her legs and feasted on her waiting womanhood.

"Honey, turn around, I want to taste you too." He moaned against her clit as she took his fully engorged shaft in her mouth. The soft wet heat of her lips and tongue was almost painfully exquisite. Her vagina began to pulse and contract, her hips thrusting against his face. He spun around, looked into her eyes and plunged his entire erection deep into her. Jan almost screamed as he took her. There was no pain, no resistance, just a wonderful feeling of fullness. She smiled at him and wrapped her legs around his back.

As he began pumping into her the impending orgasm struck. For several minutes she was unaware of anything around her. The ecstasy of total sexual release engulfed her. The pleasure he was giving her blocked out all other thoughts. Hal felt the contractions begin. He felt her feet move to the bed and the upward heaving of her hips. Her soft silken lining felt so warm and good he could not stop. Harder and faster he plunged into her spasming depths. He felt the familiar tightness as his testicles drew up, ready to release their contents.

The boat, despite its size, was rocking with their efforts. The tall mast waved back and forth, the pennant flopping. Boats around them began to rock from the waves they created. Other couples smiled, knowing what was happening on Sea Fever.

With a final thrust Hal paused, his rock-like penis deep in Jan's vagina as he erupted. Again and again she felt the hot spurts as his seed sprayed against her cervix. He lifted up again, kissed her, and whispered softly. "I love you Jan!"

"And I love you too." She replied. "And lets not ever stop doing this."

They lay in each other's arms fighting to catch their breath. Each glistened with droplets of perspiration from their efforts. As their eyes met Jan whispered. "Again?"

Tom and Kate returned at mid-morning the next day. With them came two Mexicans pushing handcarts laden with bags and boxes. Tom pointed at the bare mast where the proposal banner had hung.

"Yes, I saw that," Kate replied, a large smile on her face. The four of them were stacking supplies on the deck when Hal and Jan appeared

"What the hell is all this?" Hal demanded

Tom leaned against the cabin wall. "Well, 'all this' is food, booze, some extra equipment, and some woman stuff. "

"Well let's get it below and stowed away."

"Right Skipper, but first have a look at this" Tom handed Hal a magazine opened to a particular page.

Hal's eyes opened wide as he glimpsed a picture of a beautiful yacht. He quickly scanned the listing information

"She looks like a winner Captain. The price is a little high, but she's in Brownsville right now. We could be there in a few days."

Jan came up and peered over Hal's shoulder. Seeing the photo she whistled. "Wow! That's a pretty fancy rowboat. How much?"

"They are asking three hundred grand but I think they'll go a lot lower."

"But Tom, sixty-five feet is not a boat, it's a ship. And no sails means a lot of fuel."

"You're right again but how many cruise passengers know anything about sailing? Or want to be involved in running the boat, or ship, or whatever? People that go on dive cruises want to dive, not spend days getting to a reef on a sailboat."

" Well it says this tub will do thirty knots. Can you imagine how much fuel those two big diesels would burn at that speed?"

"But Hal, we're not going on a cruise around the world. You know as well as I do that some of the best diving in the world is within a hundred miles of here. So we load up with paying customers and an hour or so later they're in the water. Feed them a fancy meal, and a few drinks, and the next day we are at a new dive spot, maybe twenty miles away. This 'tub' as you call it has six staterooms besides the Captains cabin and the crew quarters. So six couples at Seven fifty a day for ten days comes out to what?"

"Forty five thousand dollars." Offered Jan, seeing Tom struggle to work out the figures in his head.

The other three looked at Jan. To each the number seemed incredible. "We should clear abouttwenty thousand per trip after fuel, food and expenses. Split that right down the middle and we each get five hundred a day, plus tips."

It was Hal's turn to whistle. "That's not bad at all. And I think I know who our new treasurer and accountant is going to be."

"But that is only at seven fifty a couple per day. With us supplying the diving gear, giving lessons, and PADI certification we could easily charge a grand a day.

"Whoa, hold on a minute. We don't have a boat yet. Lets put the cart back behind the horse. You guys are forgetting something. We are talking about at least a quarter of a million bucks. We will have some pretty heavy payments to make. Then there is insurance to pay for."

Kate handed Hal the cell phone. "The number is in the ad boss. So call the broker and go from there."

* * * *

By noon the following day Sea Fever was passing Cabo Catoche, the northernmost tip of Quintaneroo. From here they had over six hundred miles of open water to go direct to Brownsville, Texas. At her top sailing speed they would be seventy hours getting there. It gave them three days to think things over and make tentative plans.

By the end of the week they were rounding the southern tip of Padre Island. They dropped the sails and motored into the marina at Port Isabel.

The boat in the ad was tied up to the pier. Hal found a vacant slip and guided Sea Fever to the mooring cleats. The larger boat looked even bigger than the picture indicated. The hull was all white but showed a few rust stains.

Jan whistled," She's big, but she looks fast and comfortable."

"Let's see if we can find the broker, or the owner." Said Hal. "Then we can start going over her with a fine toothed comb.

"You know," quipped Kate. "I don't think all four of us could rock that boat."

Chapter Thirty-One

The four new partners had to wait to see the boat. The owner was out of town and the broker was busy with other prospects. Hal went into the marina office and arranged to rent a car.

"Jan and I have some shopping to do. Do you guys want to come along or do your own thing?

"You two go ahead," offered Kate. 'We have some things to take care of here."

"Well just don't rock the boat." Laughed Hal.

Jan poked him in the ribs, Tom laughed, and Kate blushed.

Hal soon found a large jewelry store and led Jan inside. With a clerk in attendance they were soon looking at a variety of rings. She finally picked out one with a tiny diamond. She tried it on, and it fit.

"Are you sure?" Asked Hal. "Honey I don't need a big rock to carry around. This set will say I am married to you. That's all I want. And it includes a band for you."

Tom was suddenly crestfallen. He held up his left hand. The little finger and the ring finger were the ones that were missing. "Sorry honey, no ring for me I'm afraid."

"Well you can wear it on the next finger. Or we could put it through your nose"

Hal waited until the clerk had gone to get a box for their purchase. "I know somewhere else I could wear it. But it would have to be made a lot bigger."

Jan blushed. "Hal be nice."

Okay, I'll be nice. But lets go back to the boat and get Tom and Kate, then go find a Justice of the Peace or a minister or something."

"Honey? Now?" She squealed.

"Well unless you want to wait a while."

* * * *

When they arrived back at the boat they found their new partners talking to an older man in a light tan suit. "Hey Skipper, you're just in time. This gentleman is the broker looking after this boat we want to see." Tom had a big smile on his face. "He says he can give us a really good deal and take Sea Fever in trade.

"Well, I guess the least we can do is have a look." The broker smiled, "I'm Fred McGinnis, my friends call me Mac." He offered his hand.

"Harold Sigurdson, Master of the Sea Fever, folks call me Hal." The two men shook hands.

"Okay Hal, well she is unlocked. You are welcome to go aboard and look around. I have a surveyor's report unless you would like to hire your own man.

"Ok Mac, Thanks, we'll have a look first and then decide." The broker handed Hal a business card and walked toward the marina office.

The Captain grabbed a couple of flashlights and headed for the big yacht. "Lets see if we can find some problems on this big rowboat."

The foursome used up the afternoon investigating the big powerboat. As arranged they met on the bridge at four o'clock to compare notes.

Hal went first. "She is not in as nice a shape as Sea Fever. There are a few things that need to be done in the staterooms. The engine room needs some cleaning but according to the logs the engines have been serviced regularly. There is some water in the bilge but there's no way of knowing when it was pumped out last."

Tom then added his information. "She has been well used for sure but if the hull and the engines are okay I think it will do nicely."

"Kate and I went through the galley," began Jan. "It needs a good cleanup and a few minor repairs but it could be an awesome place to prepare great meals."

Hal summed it up. "Well the electronics, radios and navigation equipment are getting old but they seem to work okay. The exterior is the worst, she is showing a lot of rust stains."

* * * *

The Captain put his arm around his fiance "Now there is one detail we need to get settled. Jan and I want to get married! But we don't want a big shindig. We would like you two to be our witnesses, best man and bridesmaid or whatever. It will be just a simple ceremony with a Justice or a minister or whoever it takes."

Kate smiled, a tear in her eye. "Oh Jan congratulations, of course we'll stand up for you." The two women hugged and sobbed together.

Tom grasped Hal's hand and congratulated him before giving Jan a big hug.

Hal then continued, "The next thing on the agenda is this ship. Are we going to buy it or keep looking?"

Tom voiced his opinion, "I think we should get an unbiased opinion from an expert. This thing is too big and too complicated for us to really know what we're doing. We need to check with local maintenance people, the Coast Guard, and a licensed Marine Surveyor. The last thing we need is to buy someone else's headache."

The other three agreed with Tom's suggestion. Then Jan added her thought; "But that doesn't mean we have to quit looking. There may be a better boat around for a lower price. After all, do we really need sixty-five feet?"

That afternoon they found themselves in the office of the Chief Justice. The required license had been purchased and the court official performed the ceremony. It was quick and simple but at the end Hal and Jan were man and wife. To celebrate they went out to a Texas roadhouse for dinner. The wine flowed and they devoured huge steaks and lobster tails. The conversation at the table kept coming back to the boat. Finally Tom made a suggestion;

"Hey you two, the surveyor said he couldn't have a report ready in less than a week. Kate and I have some loose ends to tie up at home. So why don't you two take Sea Fever and go on a honeymoon for a couple of weeks? When we get back we can do whatever we are going to do to get this business off the ground."

Jan looked over to Hal, smiled at him, and nodded.

Hal shrugged his shoulders. "It looks like I'm outnumbered, and it is a hell of a plan."

Tom and Kate packed their luggage into a rented car. The newlyweds made ready to set sail. The goodbyes were said.

The Wakeman's stood on the pier and watched the Sea Fever leave the harbor.

"Where do you think they'll go?" Asked Kate. Tom smiled, "I don't know, but knowing those two it won't be far. They'll be rocking the boat before nightfall."

The End

∎∎

Please see the next page for more books by
Jim Prentice

The Mysterious Disk

Fly Into Danger

Sunken Treasure

The Rum Runner

Disaster On The Tundra

Rescue 235

RV Trips, Tips,Trips and Slips

Bulls, Bears, Bullets, and Booze

Blue Sky View